COWBOY HEAVEN

COWBOY HEAVEN

Ron Goulart

DOUBLEDAY & COMPANY, INC.

GARDEN CITY, NEW YORK

1979

With the exception of actual historical persons,
all of the characters in this book are fictitious
and any resemblance to actual persons, living or
dead, is purely coincidental.

Library of Congress Cataloging in Publication Data

Goulart, Ron, 1933–
Cowboy heaven.

I. Title.
PZ4.G692Co [PS3557.O85]   813'.5'4
ISBN: 0-385-12784-7
Library of Congress Catalog Card Number 77-27672

COWBOY HEAVEN

CHAPTER

ONE

The beautiful golden-haired girl lay on the enormous pink bed, forming a naked X. "I truly feel," she sighed, "you're the most relaxing man in Hollywood, Andy. I'm looking forward to this one."

"It's actually you who helps me relax, Alicia." Andy Stoker, a long lanky man of twenty-nine, was shedding his trousers quickly. "After a day like today at Stamms-Important I'm really anticipating—"

Brtzz! Brtzz!

"Nerf!" Alicia Bramble sat abruptly up on her gigantic circular bed and grabbed a pixphone from a pink marble night table. "Bramble here. What's your nerfing problem?"

A black man appeared on the waffle-size screen. "Hunneker is going to sue."

"Nerf him. I broadcast nothing but the truth on my TV show tonight."

"He says it wasn't no wig he wore in *Love Among the Foliage*," the black man told the lovely gossip. "He says the chimp ain't no robot. He says the whole and entire story about the vacuum cleaner is no-how true."

"What about padding his loincloth? Does the big nerf deny that, too?"

"He says it's an old and honored show-business tradition for jungle men to pad their . . ."

Pulling his mesh shorts and denim trousers up again, Andy started easing toward the lemon-yellow bathroom.

"Tell Hunneker," Alicia was saying, "I've got X-ray pix of that farbing chimpanzee and he's all nuts and bolts inside."

"He swallows stuff, maintains Hunneker, which is how—"

"Don't flush," cautioned Alicia.

"Huh?" inquired her black associate.

"Talking to company. Andy, don't flush. I'm about to go

over my water quota for this week. I really can't flush until day after tomorrow."

"Was only going to hide in there," Andy said, "while you and Cleveland talk business."

"That nerfing jungle man is trying to sue us," said the lovely unclothed girl. "I don't like to interrupt a good roll in the hay anymore than you do, Andy, but I'm not about to let some farping over-the-hill king of the jungle who wears a tacky leopard skin tell me I—"

"Tiger skin," corrected Andy.

"Tiger, leopard . . . Cleveland, tell the network not to fret. We'll send them copies of everything in our Hunneker file first thing."

"The chimp," added Cleveland, "is filing a separate suit."

"He can sloop himself with a bunch of green bananas." Alicia clicked off the pixphone, smacked it once with her fist, and then stretched out languidly on the bed once more. "Being Hollywood's No. 1 gossip columnist, as well as the managing editor of *Filmfreak* magazine, is no easy cross to bear."

"Do you," asked Andy as he returned to lowering his pants, "always talk to Cleveland naked?"

"Cleveland? He's safe. I'll show you my file on him."

"You could blank your side of the call."

"For Cleveland?" She grinned, twisting a lock of golden hair slowly around her forefinger and then biting at the finger.

"Suppose it hadn't been Cleveland? Suppose it'd been . . . oh, the Westwood Strangler?"

"He doesn't have my private number," said Alicia. "And besides, he's in Vegas taping the 'Tonight' show."

Andy had himself undressed again. "We won't argue about it." He approached her bed. "Because the main purpose of our relationship is to relax each other. We want to forget our respective work, forget about—"

"So have I been reminding you of work? Did I even mention how nerfy I think it is that I have to find out about Hunneker's trying to stick a dagger into my vitals from the grapevine instead of you? The Stamms-Important Talent Agency does handle Hunneker, after all, as well as his robot chimp. But I—"

"The chimp isn't a robot. He merely happens to have a couple false parts, Alicia. He's, you know, a cyborg." Andy seated himself on the opposite edge of the immense bed. "After all, the President of the United States has a plastic heart and you don't go calling him—"

"That burp. Watch my gossip show tomorrow if you want to find out who he's been slooping. Those pious ones are the—"

"We'll talk later." He commenced working his way across the neosilk sheets to her.

"Isn't that what I just now suggested? I'm not about to razz you because you didn't even warn me what Hunneker was planning. If some senile apeman decides to plant a dirk in—"

"He isn't one of the S-I clients I handle. And he only made up his nitwit mind to sue you tonight, so—"

"You knew he wears a tiger skin instead of a leopard skin."

"Anybody knows that. I mean, it's got stripes instead of spots. Therefore—"

"I'm the managing editor of the nation's leading movie and TV mag and I didn't know it." She sat up, pressing her smooth, richly tan back against the backrest. "Nor did Cleveland Jazzbo Birmingham Brown, the ace trouble-shooter for my staff, know—"

"There's another thing." He slowed his advance toward her. "How come he's got such a racist name? You'd think a black man who—"

"What kind of name is Andy Stoker if it comes down to that? Sounds like a soft drink without sugar. Just plain Andy, mind you, not a diminutive of Andrew or Alexander or—"

"Did I tell you that?"

"It's in your file."

Andy scowled at the beautiful gossip. "You've got one of those on me?"

Sighing, Alicia puckered one cheek. "Boy, what a nerfing world this is. Here I do a terrific job of digging up dirt on every person in this slooping town and all I—"

"I'm not a damn celebrity, I'm only an agent."

"You're Jake Troop's agent," said Alicia. "Besides which, I'm honestly very fond of you. Naturally I want to know if your given name is Andrew, Anderson, or plain unimaginative Andy."

"Just ask me."

"I don't feel right grilling people I'm honestly fond of," said the girl. "For instance, when I lived with Rance Keane I never once inquired about his trigger finger being—"

"Some idiot pro gunfighter. Forget about—"

"Also, for instance, I haven't asked you to confirm the rumors I've been hearing about Jake Troop."

"No more shop talk for a while, okay?" He touched her nearest thigh with his fingertips. "What rumors?"

Smiling, Alicia spread her arms wide. "I'm not going to allude to them at all, Andy, proving beyond a doubt how honestly fond I am of you."

"He isn't drinking any longer," Andy lied. "If that's what you heard."

"A man his age," said the girl while stroking the hand that was stroking her, "a man who's been our top-grossing Western star since he made *Night Stage* ages and ages ago . . . it figures."

"What figures?"

She slithered across the slick sheets, clamped both arms tight around him. "We don't want to talk business. Any two people in this nerfing town can talk business in the sack. Our relationship is much more speci—"

"Is it his health? Have you been maybe hearing snide and untruthful rumors about Jake Troop's health?"

"Forget Jake Troop," she whispered warmly in his ear,

"forget the workaday pressures. Relax, relax, Andy, concentrate on me. Here I am, a twenty-seven-year-old girl from Glendale who now has the top-rated show-business TV show in the world, whose syndicated column runs in 846 papers around the globe, whose magazine has a 6 million circulation. Yet I don't want to have you tell me anything about Jake Troop's problems. Make love to me, Andy. Now!"

"First let me tell you, Alicia, that Jake Troop had a complete physical, head to toe, only last week and he's—"

"No more conversation." She pressed her lips against his cheek. "I'm sure *Saddle Tramp* won't lose its backers over some foolish scuttlebutt."

"He's in tip-top shape, Alicia. For a man of sixty-two he's absolutely marvelous—"

"Sixty-*five*, darling. I'll show you his file."

"I don't have to see Jake Troop's file. I ought to know his nerfing age, oughtn't I? He's my major property at Stamms-Important. He's only sixty-two."

"Do we need to quarrel over three nerfing years? Not at all." She kissed his throat, his face, his ears.

The giant oval window across the bedroom exploded inward then, and an old cowboy came somersaulting into the room.

"My god, it's Jake Troop!" Andy stood straight up in bed.

Alicia snorted. "No, it's not. It's that burp, the Sweetwater Kid. Pick him up off that hookrug, will you?"

Hopping off the bed, Andy gathered his shorts and trousers.

"Groan, moan," said the big sprawled old man in the buckskin suit.

"Come on, come on," urged Alicia, drawing a sheet up in front of her as high as the tops of her breasts. "He may be expiring; I don't want that happening all over my floor."

"Soon as I get some of my clothes on." After zipping his fly, he knelt beside the cowboy.

"Doggone, I got to get me some of the psychiatric help." The Sweetwater Kid pushed himself up into a kneeling position. "Dadburn if I can shake the habit of coming into a room via the window. If you remember my moving pictures you know that was exact how I done it then, sort of a trademark it was."

"Nope, I don't remember your movies. I thought you were Jake Troop."

"Shucks, I don't look nothing like old Trooper."

"You're the same general size. I guess I had Jake Troop on my mind."

"Honest to my granny, if I was in bed with a filly like Alicia Bramble, I sure wouldn't not be thinking 'bout old Trooper." Wobbling, boots digging zigzag patterns into the rug, the Kid got to his feet. "Course you never never know what I'm like to get in my head. Plum loco I am sometimes. Too much stunt work."

Alicia asked, "What did you want, Kid?"

"I missed you at the dingbust office you got down to

the Strip, honey," explained the large old cowboy, tipping his dented Stetson. "I sorely wished, though, to deliver you a publicity kit in person." He reached under his buckskin shirt. "Darned if I ain't thirstier than a maverick in a dust storm after my little impromptu stunt. Would you have—"

"No liquor," said Alicia.

"I'd settle for only a glass of—"

"No water," she said.

"Not until day after tomorrow," added Andy.

"Can't get used to all this here-now rationing." The Sweetwater Kid produced a stiff-cover folder, waved it absently in the air. "When we was shooting them Westerns of mine seemed like it rained hereabouts ever dang day. I used to say as much to Benny, who was my horse. Tom Mix had Tony, Ken Maynard had Tarzan, I had Benny."

"There's the reason you were such a flop," said the lovely columnist. "Nobody gives a nerf for a guy with a horse named Benny."

"Listen, missy, that dang horse pulled more fan mail than me. They was going to put his hoofprints, all four of them, in cement in front of Grauman's Chinese except the critter come down with a bad case of—"

"Hand over the publicity stuff, Kid, then take a jump out of here."

Chuckling, the old stuntman squinted at the ruined window. "Does make a nice entrance, don't it? You remember in *Bells of Laguna Honda* when Pedro the greaser is about to—"

"You ought to give Andy a kit, too," cut in the girl. "He's Jake Troop's talent rep over at S-I."

"Doggone, ain't that a coincidence." The Kid slapped his thigh with his hat. "I been trying to set up a meeting with you. So as we can work out all the final details."

"Details?" Andy decided to put on his shirt.

"Shucks, I'm doing ever'thing backward again. See, I'm the public-relations director for Cowboy Heaven," said the Sweetwater Kid. "That's the big movie cowboy memorabilia museum opening down in Drywell, Texas, next month."

"You ought to know about that, Andy," said Alicia wth a smile. "Jake Troop is slated to be the guest of honor."

"Yeah, I know. I'll be traveling down there with him," he said. "Don't know why we haven't met before, Kid."

"Aw, that must be on account of I been laid up for a spell 'count of that incident at the Aquatic Baptist Church in Santa Monica," said the old cowboy. "Made one of my typical entrances, but doggone if them stained-glass windows ain't buggers. Got lead in them or something. I'm only just now up and around and doing my PR chores."

"We'll take two kits," said Alicia, "then you can leave, Kid."

"Here you go, little missy." He fetched a second folder from inside his clothes and, with a bow, placed them atop the nearest pink table. "I'll drop in on you during regular business hours, Andrew."

"Listen, I'm up on the thirtieth floor of the Stamms-Important Building, so perhaps you better not try entering by way of the—"

"Aw don't you fret none. I'm making a real effort to overcome my little quirk." He strode, spurs jingling, to the broken window. Slapping his Stetson back on his gray head, the Sweetwater Kid leaped out into the night.

"Actors." Alicia let the sheet drop away.

Andy said nothing. He stood fiddling with a button of his shirt.

"Jake Troop will be well enough to attend the Cowboy Heaven ceremonies," said Alicia, "won't he?"

"Sure. Since there's absolutely nothing wrong with him," he said. "Say Alicia, would you mind if I left now? What with phone calls and cowboys coming in at the windows . . . I seem to have lost my incentive."

Alicia shrugged, tossing her long blond hair. "Want to check up on Jake Troop once more tonight? You can use my phone if you like."

"No, it's not that. There's nothing wrong with Jake." He located his socks and his shoes, upended the shoes to shake out any glass fragments they might have caught. "Actually I'm somewhat old-fashioned, Alicia. Making love in a room with a missing window makes me self—"

"This is," the naked girl reminded, "a twenty-six-room mansion I got here."

"Bedroom," said Andy. "I always like to make love in a bedroom, some sort of quirk."

"I have five other bedrooms."

"Even so." Fully dressed, he circled the mammoth bed to kiss Alicia once on her warm forehead. "Lunch tomorrow?"

"Can't."

"Neither can I, matter of fact. So I'll phone you. Night."

"Night, sweet."

Outside in the garage area the sky showed surprisingly clear. You could see stars, not many but some. "Jake Troop, Jake Troop," Andy muttered to himself. "That nerf is fouling up my whole and entire life." He slid into his Nezumi sports car. "And how the hell did Alicia find out he was laid up?"

He drove, too fast, to his boss's house in Bel Air.

CHAPTER TWO

"Spare a buck?" The ragged man came tottering out of the dry shrubbery.

"Evening, Catman. Is she home?"

Catman straightened, yanked off his tattered tennis hat. "You tumbled it was me right off, huh, Stoker?"

"Don't see too many panhandlers in this part of Bel

Air." Andy continued walking up the wide gravel pathway.

Catman, wincing and muttering, plucked the imitation stubble from his cheeks. "I'm sure not going to make a comeback as a hero," he said. "It follows I've got to establish myself as a character man."

"You need a broader base to operate from. Working in the bushes here at Novella's mansion you—"

"She's always got some noted filmland celeb calling on her," said Catman as he accompanied him to the door of the Moorish-style mansion. "Why, tonight we've had visits from Oslo Huckleburg, Whistlin' Pete Goodwin, Twitchy Ploog, and Sky Lancer. Burns Prine is in there right now."

Andy frowned. "Thought that was his Mercedes I parked next to. What's he want?"

"Couldn't say." Catman shook his head. "He got to explaining to me what was wrong with my Irish grandmother and thus we—"

"You don't have an Irish grandmother."

"No, no, I *was* an Irish grandmother. That's the character bit I was trying out when I let Prine in tonight," the large fifty-two-year-old actor said. "Imagine that, Catman going around in drag. Quite a comedown." He bounded up the red-tile porch to pull open the door for Andy. "It's running in Kecskemet, Hungary, now, Stoker. Next month Legnica, Poland, is picking it up."

"Your old 'Catman' television show, you mean?"

Nodding, the former hero said "Who could have fore-

seen such a turn of events? Not me. Not Novella. What a
lousy contract we signed with Jarndyce Productions. The
damn thing is on every day, even Sundays, in Trivan-
drum, India, and we don't see penny one. Over in Wad
Medani in the Sudan they recently ran the first thirteen
segs back to back and—"

"You ought to talk to Novella again." Andy crossed the
threshold into the immense tile-floored hallway.

"She doesn't really want me to thrive is what I suspect,"
Catman confided. "I'm too good a butler. That's always
been my problem, Stoker, I really get into a part. I *was*
Catman and now I really am Novella Stamms' butler.
Sometimes in this town it's bad when you're too terrific."

"I know," said Andy as the forlorn butler shut him in
the house.

Years ago—more than sixty, in fact—this place had
belonged to Udolpho Otranto, the famous silent-screen
lover. Tiny portraits of the Latin actor were still dimly
visible in the tiles of the hallway, hundreds of profiles
stretching from here to the wrought-iron and glass music
room at the rear of the big house. When Bunny & Slick,
the momentarily famous rock team of the distant 1960s,
occupied the mansion, an effort to replace some of the
Otranto tiles had been made. When Andy was crossing
the stretch of glow-color tiles he heard Novella's angry
voice echoing out in the music room.

"Do these ears deceive me, schmuck? Or are you indeed evading an answer to my question?"

"There's no need to scream, Novella. I'm only being cautious."

"This is hardly, may I point out, the time for caution. Is the old SOB dead or alive?"

"You've made anger one of your business tools for so long, Novella, that you—"

"Would you two be discussing Jake Troop?" Andy hesitated at the open doorway. "I hope not, because if he's dead I'm going to have a hell of a time with the Sweetwater Kid and—"

"Jake is very much alive," said Burns Prine. He was a slim young man, a good many years from thirty, wearing a synhide suit of rusty brown and sitting, very relaxed, in a metal chair across the large hollow room.

Novella, as usual, was wandering around, kicking at things, poking spots on the metal furniture and the pianos. A hefty woman, her hair a bluish blonde, she was sixty-one years old. Her pinstripe jumpsuit was of a nubby pseudotweed. "Ah young Stoker, what brings you calling at this unseemly hour, may I ask?"

"There are a lot of negative rumors floating around out there, Novella." He, very tentatively, went into the room. "I thought we'd kept that little heart attack of Jake's last month a secret."

Fisting a few bass keys on one of the pianos, Novella said, "It's a most interesting coincidence, your dropping in here like this. For only moments ago I endeavored to contact you at the home of that goldilocks bimbo you cohabit with."

"I'm not cohabiting with Alicia Bramble," corrected Andy. "Nobody could actually, there's too damn much chaos for—"

"One would think a young person with such a lamentably meager bosom would refrain from answering the pixphone in an unclad state."

"A bad habit of Alicia's, I have to admit. Now, Novella, what's wrong with Jake Troop this time? I continue to—"

"There's hardly anything wrong with Jake," said young Prine, who was the veteran cowboy actor's personal business manager. "He's merely suffered another very mild—"

"When I was the most sought-after cheesecake model in the country, one is tempted to say the world," said Novella, rubbing dust specks from a glass-top table, "I had a bosom which both delighted and astounded my numerous admirers. Yet I never dreamed, had we enjoyed pixphones in the days when I was gracing the glossy pages of *Lace Nightie, Garter Belt, Black Frilly Underthings, Pink Rubber*—"

"Suffered?" Andy approached the seated business manager. "What has Jake Troop suffered this time?"

"Nothing much, Andy, really. Another little heart attack is all."

"Another little heart attack?" He sank down onto a piano stool. "How can he keep having heart attacks, anyway? I thought the plastic heart you guys bought him two years ago was supposed to—"

"Even a mechanical heart can go on the fritz once in a

while, Andy," Prine patiently explained. "An active guy like Jake, it's difficult persuading him to—"

"Out the window," said Novella. "Jake propelled two of his minions out a window, as I am given to understand the matter." She ceased her pacing, faced Prine with her hands locked behind her. "I needn't, one may assume, remind you what a hump-busting time we had getting together the $8 million for *Saddle Tramp*. Indeed, even now one has some foreboding about the position of the Crocker-Arab Bank. And you may as well know, should you not as yet have heard, that Mr. Achraq of the Morgan-Mohammed Bank & Trust has been trying to reach me on the phone all day."

"I'm aware of all this, Novella. After all, you people only put this package together. I'm the one who's doing the actual—"

"Okay, enough schmuck talk," she said. "When I merged with Famous & Important back in the seventies I assured all the people one of the things I would do was make Jake Troop a hot property again. Only an innate modesty prevents me from crowing over the abundant success of that particular vow. *Rio Cholo* has grossed 19 million bucks to date. *Lonesome Cowboy* isn't far behind with—"

"Novella, I only dropped in to inform you Jake's had a very unimportant heart attack." Prine rose out of his chair. "Unlike some of those who're involved with the fortunes of Jake Troop, I'm always honest and open with everyone."

"Ha," said Novella.

"You really ought to think about practicing moderation, Novella. Or one of these days you're going to—"

"Moderation didn't make S-I the biggest talent packager in the world, schtoop. Moderation didn't make Mrs. Stamms' little girl the king of the mountain." She jabbed a finger at him. "We're going to see Jake."

Prine ran his tongue over his lips. "Of course, Novella. Just as soon as—"

"Not just as soon as anything, putz. Tonight."

"I really wouldn't advise that. The doctor's given me strict instructions to—"

"Might I suggest you and the medical man avail yourselves of a flying leap at the hole in a rolling donut?" She strode across the music room, caught hold of Andy's arm. "Come along, you'll drive me out there now."

"Buckaroo Ranch?"

"That's where Jake is."

"That place really unsettles me, Novella, and I feel—"

"You'll feel even worse, my lad, attempting to sell rainmakers door to door in the wastes of San Fernando Valley. When you work for Novella Stamms you work for Novella Stamms."

Andy allowed her to escort him out of the room.

CHAPTER
THREE

"Should he be making those noises inside him, doctor?"

"Merely a little flatulence, young lady."

"Flatulence doesn't hum. That's a humming I hear."

"With any imitation heart you have to learn to expect—"

"Shoo, scram, get along! Both of you!" Jake Troop sat up in the redwood bed, taking a swing at the rumpled doctor who was hovering over him. With his other rough hand he shoved the raven-haired girl off the edge of the bed. "Evening, Novella. How are you, Andy, old buckaroo?"

" 'How are you?' is the germane inquiry," said Novella Stamms while crossing the large beam-ceilinged bedroom.

"Aw I'm doggone fine. Just 'cause a sawbones comes sad-facing around . . . Rita, I told you not to light on me no more." He punched the dark girl in the backside she'd been in the process of lowering to the bed.

"I still don't believe you should be humming so loud inside you, Jake." Rita backed toward one of the Navajo blanket wall hangings.

"Have you met my latest quack, Novella?"

The fat rumpled man said, "I'm Dr. Faustus, and no jokes about my name, please. Lord knows I hear enough of them from my—"

"How serious is it this time, Jake?" Novella asked the massive cowboy star.

"Aw it's only a little bitty heart seizure," replied Troop with that familiar quirky grin of his. "I was rough-housing some with Crabby and a couple of the Tumbleweed Boys when I felt a tiny twinge across—"

"A serious malfunction," said Dr. Faustus, poking his fists into the lumpy pockets of his coat. "The equivalent of a massive heart attack if your heart were still real, Jake. You absolutely must—"

"Can you believe any of this, Novella? Now Crabby is

seventy-two and most of the Tumbleweed Boys are over sixty and yet I couldn't even toss them around much without causing my new heart to act funny. Doggone, we paid $70,000 for the thing."

"A man your age," said the doctor, "can't have these angry episodes without expecting—"

"I wasn't angry, you doggone quack." Troop sat up. "When Jake Troop is angry there ain't no doubt about it. If you money-grubbing waddies hadn't sold me a defective pump in the first place I—"

"You have a Nezumi heart, Jake. They're the best in the world, the most carefully tested. Why, before each one is installed—"

"You look, you'll forgive my mentioning, terrible," Novella told the cowboy.

"I've always looked terrible, honey. That's part of my box-office charm. Remember what the *Village Voice* said about me once? 'A craggy visage which hints of origin in a block of stone or an ageless mesa, Jake's face conveys untold—'"

"I mean terrible in the medical sense, schmuck."

A redwood door opened and Burns Prine, panting very discreetly, entered the sickroom. "You really drive at an insane pace, Andy."

"That was actually Novella," explained Andy.

"I saw you in the driver's seat."

"Yeah, but she always puts her foot on the gas pedal over mine when she's in a hurry."

"Come on, honey," said the big cowboy to Novella,

"I'm as sound as a . . ." He commenced swaying, grabbed at air, and thunked back against a bedpost. "Doggone, got woozy there for a second."

"I better listen to that chest again." Dr. Faustus patted his pockets in search of his stethoscope. "Don't punch me when I approach you."

"Be sure you stick the right part in your ear this time," said Troop. "Rita, will you wheel the portable bar in from the rumpus room?"

"Jake, you're not supposed to—"

"Nagging is not one of the things I keep you around for." Troop struggled to a more upright position in bed. "Wheel that nerfing thing in here before I hop out of here and swat your tail."

The girl glanced from the swaying cowboy to the doctor. "Dr. Faustus?"

"No booze." He inserted the earpieces in his ears.

"Listen, you wall-eyed buffoon, when Jake Troop wants a glass of ale . . ." He sank back suddenly. "Doggone, doc, she's right. I'm making all kinds of funny noises inside me."

"What can you expect?" The fat doctor listened to Troop's wide chest. "You put too much strain on it, a mechanical heart isn't meant—"

"Seventy-thousand bucks and I still can't have a drink when I want or throw a few good-natured punches."

Andy moved nearer to the cowboy's young business manager. "Jake's going to be able to attend the opening of Cowboy Heaven, isn't he?"

"Certainly he is, Andy. I've never worked with such gloomy people. This is one tough hombre you're looking at. He did all his own stunts in *Wagon Wheels Westward*, didn't he?"

"Which is why he had to get the plastic heart in the first place," reminded Andy. "I'm seriously worried, Burns. Escorting Jake down to Drywell, Texas, even when he's in good shape would be an ordeal . . . but the shape he's in now." He shook his head.

"It shouldn't be ratcheting, Jake," said the concerned Rita. "Humming is maybe okay, but not ratchety-ratchety."

"Shut up a minute, honey," advised Troop.

"The noises are rather worrisome," said the doctor. "Whir-whir thunka-thunka razzle-razzle. Blurtz whir-whir thunka-thunka razzle-razzle. Worrisome."

"It isn't exactly razzle-razzle," said Rita. "It's more ratchety-ratchety."

"My dear, I am the medical man here. Suffice it to say I know a ratchety-ratchety from a razzle-razzle. I recall a case in—"

"Doc, I think I'd like me a snooze." Perspiration had formed on Troop's weathered forehead. The big hand he wiped it off with quivered slightly. "Whyn't you and everybody clear on out of my boudoir."

"A very good idea. Rest may be exactly what's called for."

"Course it is, you lop-eared walrus." Troop dropped his head down on his pillow, eyes snapping shut. "No need to fret none, Novella," he murmured. "I'll be back in the saddle by the first of next week. Plenty of time to jaunt down to Cowboy Heaven. . . ."

Out in the living room again Andy said, "There goes *Saddle Tramp*. If anyone sees Jake in that state we're finished, the backing will dry up. Nobody'll fund the picture, the insurance company'll—"

"Everything will, mark my words, work out," Novella announced.

Easing into a redwood chair, Burns Prine said, "You're sounding surprisingly optimistic, Novella. Can't tell you how pleased that makes me."

"Why is anybody optimistic?" asked Andy, staring at both of them. "Jake Troop's flat on his can with a heart that makes noise like a rusty New Year's Eve party favor. If I don't show off a hale and hearty Jake Troop in Drywell, Texas, next month we can kiss—"

"A hale and hearty Jake Troop will be there, rest assured," said the hefty Novella.

"How can you be anyway certain about that? You just remarked how awful he looks."

"It's time," said Novella, "to tell you about Dr. Mackinson."

"Dr. Mackinson? Who's he?"

Prine straightened up. "There's absolutely no need to resort to such—"

"Quiet, schmuck," said Novella.

CHAPTER

FOUR

The sunburned man at the next table slumped, the left side of his face slapped down into his plate of mock knockwurst. Trailing whips of mock sauerkraut, he continued down to smack into the tiled floor of the bright outdoor restaurant terrace.

"Beautiful, lovely." A small jumpy man in a one-piece

rayon suit trotted over, squatting beside the fallen man. Into a portable dictating machine he began chanting, "Nuke Nultz, two-fisted box-office dynamite, whose fillum *Blotch* is being touted for many Oscars, did a floppo from too many druggos the other midday at movietown's new fave Mock's on—"

"He's only drunk, Harlo," said the stunning black girl who was the unconscious actor's lunch partner. "And why don't you pick the poor boy up?"

"You pick him up, Bimba, he's your frapping date, sweetie." Into his handmike Harlo Glasspants said, "Looks like, from where I'm sitting, like the torrid romance between Nultz and thirteen-year-old stagflick sensation Marina Graustark is going flooey because—"

"At least get your knee offen him." Bimba had come around to attempt to revive Nultz.

"This isn't," said Andy in a low voice, "exactly the best place in Hollywood for a private talk, Huck."

Across the small circular lucite table sat Huck Levitz, a middle-size, curly-haired man of thirty-one. He happened to be Andy's only close friend at the Stamms-Important Talent Agency. "Didn't realize you wanted real privacy," he said, watching the pretty black girl bend Nuke Nultz up into a sitting posture. "Usually you're anxious to plant something in Harlo's column."

"No, not today. Today I—"

"An item?" Harlo, his small mouth attempting a smile, was now hovering beside them. "Got something for me, Andy? What's this I hear about you last night?"

Andy concentrated on slicing his mock T-bone. "Last night?"

"You punched the Sweetwater Kid, onetime cinema somebody, on the snoot when the wiseguy made nasty noises at your No. 1 heartburn, Alicia Bramble, alleged Hollywood gossip. Decked the aging cowpoke with one bop to the—"

"Alicia and I are just friends," said Andy. "So are the Kid and I. You know how he is, very fond of entering through windows. Well, as to last night—"

"Son of a gun!" Harlo pointed excitedly across the crowded terrace. "There's world-renowned Italian director person Glory Ratwaller, whose *Six Stomach Aches* has got bigtown critics going goofy . . . and darned if she isn't sharing a menu with controversial head doctor Dr. Rollo Blurry, peppery proponent of the new Punch Therapy. Must chat." The little columnist went trotting off.

"Read Blurry's book?" asked Huck.

"What book?"

"*When I Punch Somebody in the Snoot I Feel Guilty*. Blurry maintains it's perfectly healthy to—"

Bop!

Huck raised up slightly off his chair. "Dr. Blurry just punched Harlo in the nose. Very gratifying." He sat down. "Now what about the private conversation you wanted to have?"

"Well, this is sort of—"

"I don't want to drink it," Bimba was shouting at a waiter. "I want to pour it over poor Nuke."

"Makes no difference, miss. No water."

"Everything all right at this table?" The waiter turned his attention to Andy and Huck. "And, yes, I am. I know you've been wanting to ask." He touched at the dark rings drawn around his wide eyes.

"You are what?" asked Levitz.

"People continually ask if I'm Stooge McAlpin. I am."

"Never heard of you," said Andy. "Go away."

"Sure you did. Back in the Seventies I fronted the hottest punk rock group in the world."

"That explains the sequins all over your chest," said Levitz.

"Had the little buggers implanted. No way to get them off short of surgery. The eye shadows are tattooed. You know, when you're on top you think it's never going to end." He nudged Andy. "You going to sit there and tell me you never heard of me and my group? Stooge McAlpin & Terminal Cancer?"

"I suppose I did."

"Millions of people wrote to tell us they always played our tapes while they made love. An especial favorite for cohabitation was our *Eye-gouging Mama, Come Home,* while another—"

"I was married then, I think," said Andy. "Yeah, that's right. My wife demanded absolute silence during any romantic interlude. Once I lost control to the point of crying out, 'I love you,' during an encounter and she . . . but why am I telling this to a waiter?"

"It's okay, most people find me a very sympathetic listener. Surprising for one with . . . Hey! Excuse me."

Across Mock's sun-bright terrace Dr. Blurry had taken to punching Glory Ratwaller. The waiter ran over to intervene.

"Everybody used to be something else," remarked Levitz. "That's what's so fascinating about living in the West. You rarely run into any has-beens in Bridgeport, Connecticut, where I was—"

"What do you know about robotics?" Andy asked him.

"The science of making robots. Don't tell me Alicia's item about Hunneker's chimpanzee is true?"

"This is something entirely . . . well, it's . . . you know what an android is, don't you? A robot who looks like a human being."

"Like a human and not a monkey?"

Andy made an exasperated noise before continuing. "Novella is sending me up to Berkeley tomorrow. There's a guy up there who—"

"What an odd sensation," Nuke Nultz said from the floor. "I feel just as though I'd fallen out of my chair, hit my plate with my face, and then dropped onto the floor. What happened, Bimba?"

"You fell out of your chair, hit your plate with your face, and dropped onto the floor." She dapped mock kraut from his cheek with a plyonap. "Listen, lover, you really going to have to stop with the liquor."

"This isn't liquor." The handsome actor stood with the

aid of his stunning black companion. "Didn't I join AA? I even taped that spot for them. Great stuff, we got Glory Ratwaller to direct. First pseudorealismo commercial ever to hit the tube."

"If you ain't drunk and you ain't drugged, Nuke, why'd you fall down?"

"Oh it's that electric brain stimulator I got last Christmas, Bimba. Think I must be using it turned on too high."

Elbows on table, Andy resumed. "There's this guy up in Berkeley named Dr. Mackinson. Dr. Jack Mackinson. Ever hear of him?"

"Who'd he used to be?"

"You really are a wiseacre at times, Huck."

"All the time," said his curly-haired friend. "If you want a sob sister to tell your troubles to, check back in with Alicia."

"Christ, I can't tell her any of this. If Alicia ever finds out any of this, it'll ruin everything." Andy shook his head. "Probably I won't even be able to see her for the time being. It's going to be rough."

"Torn between ass and duty, that is rough."

Andy pushed his chair back. "Come on, Huck, I'm serious. This is a dilemma."

"Having known you for six years, Andy, I'm not as shaken by these dilemmas as you are. You average about one a week."

"But this is a serious dilemma, an important one."

"Okay, so tell me."

"Maybe I should consult Dr. Blurry. There are several people I'd like to punch."

"Tell me about Dr. Mackinson," invited his friend.

"That's his specialty."

"Punching people?"

"Robotics. Making androids." Andy's head hunkered into his shoulders. "This Mackinson makes androids."

"I thought Texas Instruments and IBM and ITT made whatever robots and androids got made."

"So does everybody. Dr. Mackinson is by way of being a clandestine operator," explained Andy. "See, if you're a satisfied client of his, nobody knows it."

Levitz sat back, snapped his fingers. "He's going to build you an android replica of Jake Troop."

"Don't yell things like that," said Andy, glancing around. "Anyway, Mackinson has already actually made the damn thing. According to Novella it not only looks just like Jake Troop, it talks and acts like him, too."

"Wouldn't think there'd be much market for a machine like that."

Andy said, "Jake isn't going to be able to travel to the Cowboy Heaven opening. So I am supposed to escort this android, this mechanical man, down there and hope it fools everybody. Jake meanwhile will hide out at Buckaroo Ranch."

"Never done it myself, but I imagine it must take time to construct a robot," said Levitz. "Meaning Novella placed her order a while ago."

"Ever since Jake got the fake heart Novella's been con-

cerned. Jake Troop is still a valuable property, so long as
nobody thinks he's going to kick off in the middle of a
production. You remember how the Preiss Brothers lost
close to 4 million when Macho Knerr dropped dead a
third into *Primal Ooze?*"

"What's your immediate job?"

"I have to go up to Berkeley tomorrow, spend a few
days learning how to look after the android," said Andy.
"Then I bring him back here and we hide him until it's
time to go to the gala events down in Drywell, Texas."

"You're not happy."

"I got some qualms. I know using this machine will
solve some of S-I's problems, but basically this is a hoax, a
deception. Something that isn't honest."

"You're right, the whole idea is a dishonest one," agreed
his friend. "If it bothers you that much, quit. Quit right
now."

"Quit? How can I do that? Who'll make the payments
on my house in Beverly Glen, who'll make the tuition
payments to the Pasadena School of Anthropology I
agreed to as part of the divorce contract, who'll be able to
afford courting the likes of Alicia Bramble? Not me without a job."

"Material stuff."

"Even so."

"Okay, you can't quit. The only alternative is to go
ahead."

"There should be some other choices."

"Maybe you ought to go over and chat with Dr. Blurry.

He's probably better at the kind of advice you think you need than I am."

Andy looked across the terrace. "I won't even be able to do that. They're just carrying Dr. Blurry out on a stretcher," he said.

CHAPTER

FIVE

The raindance was blocking traffic in all directions.

Andy poked his head out of his car window into the late afternoon. A single drop of rain fell down to smack into his left eye. "They'll have to do better than that," he said to himself.

There were about thirty Indians involved in the actual

ceremony. Befeathered, masked, and painted, they danced in a wide circle around the stadium parking lot. Drums were beating, nasal voices chanted. It all seemed pretty authentic, like something out of a Jake Troop movie.

The people watching the dance, three hundred at least and mostly students at the University of California/Berkeley Division, were what was making it impossible to use any of the surrounding streets. They spilled out of the parking area next to the old football arena, milled in the streets, climbed phone poles, hopped up and down, shouted and applauded and laughed.

Sunshine McBernie wasn't helping either. His sound truck was parked directly across the road Andy wanted to drive up to get to the hillside home of the android maker he was seeking.

"This'll go on every day in Sacramento when I'm elected!" the huge black man announced. "We gone have rain dances till this great Golden State blooms again. You got the word of Sunshine McBernie on that."

"Sunshine for Gov!"

"Sunshine makes rain!"

"Water! Water!"

"I ain't just some other actor trying to jive you." McBernie was atop the yellow vehicle now, standing erect and tipping the dented derby that was his trademark. "I is a dedicated man and when I is governor of this great but parched state I tell you we gone have all the water we needs!"

"Ay Sunshine!"

"Water! Water!"

"Now when I was a child star in them famous *Us Boys* comedies," McBernie's voice boomed, "and as you all no doubt recall I portrayed the immortal Little Shoepolish, I got to admit I tommed some. But I don't jive nobody no more, folks. And I is also the only gubernatorial candidate with a 100 per cent American Indian for a lieutenant governor. When I promises you rain dances in your state capital I am gonna give them to you with real Indians. You gets no crap from Sunshine McBernie."

"No crap!"

"Ray for Sunny!"

"Water! Water!"

Andy all at once noticed a clear spot in the throng and drove his little Japanese sports car off the street and into an alley. The alley twisted and turned, coming out on an uncrowded street. There was, however, an impressively large St. Bernard dog resting in the middle of his way. He honked his horn.

The dog's big tongue unfurled some, but it remained spread out in the narrow road.

"Begone," he suggested out at it. "Go chase a cat. Go rescue a mountain climber. Get out of here."

"Darn, did he run down again?" An old bewhiskered man in a blue-and-gold collegiate-style sweater of another era came shuffling out into the street.

"No, I didn't run him down." Andy killed his engine, swung out of the Nezumi. "He was like that when—"

"Oh no, it's not your fault. I merely meant Bolivar needs rewinding." The old man produced a large silvery key, stuck it into a slot in the dog's skull, and twisted.

"That's not a real dog."

"Hardly. Couldn't wind up a real-to-goodness St. Bernard, could you?" The winding made considerable ratcheting. "This is an exact replica of our onetime house mascot. Bolivar passed on way back in '77."

Andy noticed the white-painted Victorian house this old collegian had emerged from. A sign on its porch read: *Alumni Village.* "What sort of place is that you live in?"

"I don't live there, only visit." He dropped the key into a pocket of his white duck trousers. "I'm Nogo Tarpshield, retired chairman of the board of TechPonics International. Once a year, when there's a certain tang in the air, I come back to the campus and spend a week or so at—"

"Growff growff." Bolivar was on his feet, inspecting Andy.

Tarpshield chuckled. "He's harmless. Even if he did decide to take a nip at you, which is extremely unlikely, his teeth are rubberoid. Dr. Mackinson designed him that way so—"

"Dr. Mackinson?"

"Do you know him?"

"Oh no. Actually I don't. I was thinking of a doctor my aunt used to consult, but actually I think his name was MacIntosh. Yes, Curly MacIntosh. He never manufactured robot dogs."

"That's Dr. Mackinson's specialty. He's noted far and wide for his work."

Splendid. Nothing like having a notorious robotmaker build your fake Jake Troop for you. "Does he," asked Andy casually, "manufacture people, too?"

The old alum shook his head. "Not that I know of," he said. "The big boys handle that sort of thing. Care for a brew?"

"Beg pardon?"

"A bit of college jargon from my era. I was inviting you into the house for a beer."

"Thanks, but I have several errands to run before nightfall."

"Growff growff."

"See what I mean about the rubber teeth?"

"Yep." Andy extracted his wrist from the synthetic St. Bernard's maw. "Hardly penetrated the skin."

"With a toy dog like Bolivar you never have to worry about rabies."

"That is a comfort." He climbed back into his car, started it, and drove on.

————◆————

It rained for almost two minutes.

"If McBernie can keep this up he may have a chance at getting elected after all," thought Andy as he crossed the weedy front yard.

Dr. Mackinson's two-story shingle house stood on a lop-sided lot high up on Panoramic Way. Beyond his house the land dropped away. You could see a good part of the town and a portion of San Francisco Bay framing it.

"Rainy days always make me so sad. Don't they you?" An incredibly lovely Chinese girl had opened the redwood door before he quite reached it. She was wearing a scarlet warmup suit, the jacket completely open to reveal an absence of bra. "Curl up before a roaring fire, sip brandy, read frightening tales is what I crave doing on a rainy day. To get rid of the rainy-day blues. How about you?"

"Takes a little more rain to do that to me. Five or ten minutes of steady downpour at least. I'm Andy Stoker."

"Yes, I know. I've been studying your photo in the doctor's dossiers."

"Geeze, everybody's got files."

"My name is Lana Woo. Come in. I'm not his mistress, despite any indications to the contrary. Merely his devoted assistant."

The parlor she ushered him into was paneled in dark wood. There was a deep shadowy fireplace with no fire in it. "I didn't know you had company."

"We don't. This is only the Dead End Kids."

A selection of tough, scruffy youths were seated around the parlor. "Androids, you mean?"

"A sentimental Mafia don in Arizona ordered them," said the Chinese girl. "We'll be shipping them off soon as a few kinks are worked out."

"Oh yeah?" One of the androids stood up, spit on the rug and slumped back into his wicker chair.

"We're experiencing a bit of a problem with Leo Gorcey," Lana went on. "He tends to spit at inappropriate times."

Skirting the mechanical Dead End Kids, Andy crossed to the parlor's single window and looked out its pebbled, tinted panes. "I hope the mechanism you built for—"

"Well sir, if it ain't Andy Stoker. How the heck are you, buckaroo?"

Andy spun to see Jake Troop amble into the room. "Jake, you ought to be in bed recoop . . ." Words trailing off, he approached the big cowboy. "That is you, isn't it, Jake?"

"I'm complimented, Mr. Stoker." A tall, Lincolnesque man pushed the Jake Troop simulacre aside to enter the parlor. "He is quite convincing."

Andy sniffed the air. "This isn't Jake Troop, it's your gadget?"

"Exactly."

"He smells like Jake. He even seems to be slightly drunk on ale."

"For all practical purposes, he is." Dr. Mackinson came over to Lana, patted her left buttock once. "You see, Mr. Stoker, the big boys in robotics haven't as yet succeeded in creating any really believable androids. Why, you ask? Timidity, I answer. Yes, they're afraid to program in the warts, the frailties, the little eccentricities that make up an individual personality. Not so with me. This mechanism you see before you is an *exact* replica of Jake Troop."

"Cripes," said Andy. "Now I've got two of them to worry about."

CHAPTER
SIX

Andy squatted beside the work table, attempting to look the detached android head in the eye. "This somewhat resembles Secretary of State Fassbarker," he remarked.

"Why, thank you," said Dr. Mackinson. It was dark outside the robotics laboratory, a faint wind brushed dry branches against the frosted panes of the large, long second-floor room. "I always enjoy having my work appreciated."

Straightening, Andy asked, "You mean it is supposed to be Fassbarker?"

"Most of his body's over here." The lean doctor hefted a naked torso off a tangle of spare parts, wires, twists of paper. "Very difficult job, this particular simulacre. Fassbarker was in the Navy in his youth and we've had to duplicate several intricate tattoos. Lana is very good at this sort of work, by the way, should you ever be in need of a tattoo."

"Don't think I will. Who ordered an android copy of the Secretary of State?"

"Top secret," replied Mackinson. "Shouldn't even have shown you this much. Notice how Lana exactly duplicated the rearing sea serpent here beneath Fassbarker's left nipple."

"I've never seen the Secretary of State's left nipple. What I'm curious about is why anyone would—"

"Where GAF and GE go wrong, they have an uncontrollable impulse to *improve* on nature. Not us." Mackinson's gnarled fingers traced the twisting tattoo on the chest of the android. "We duplicate every blemish, physical and mental. When all the data on Secretary Fassbarker were accumulated there was of course a temptation to improve him. Why not, for instance, fix the perspective on this dreadful battleship? Why not improve his lower anatomy so the left didn't hang so much lower than the right? Why not wipe out that tendency toward paranoia evident in his brain-scan charts? No, we resisted. Because what is called for here is an *exact* copy of—"

"It wouldn't be right for an android to sit in the President's Cabinet. I mean, that goes against all the—"

"Mr. Stoker, when you make androids you must be somewhat godlike in attitude," said Mackinson, rubbing at his Lincolnesque beard. "I create these people, I do not pass judgment. What they are used for is no concern of mine. If I did enter into the moral area I might also question the uses to which you intend to put Jake-2."

"It isn't the same thing. We're only planning to con a few investors, mostly Arabs with billions of petro-dollars. It isn't the same thing as allowing a machine to make top-level decisions which might—"

"As I say, I *don't* make moral judgments. So there is no need to convince me of anything." Dr. Mackinson perched on a metal-legged stool. "Before we join Jake-2 and Lana down in the family room, Mr. Stoker, I want to give you this brief tour of my facility and explain the ways in which my product differs from that of the biggies in the android and robot field. You didn't comment on the dinner, by the way. Did you enjoy it?"

"Sure, everything was splendid. Only dining with Jake . . . even with Jake-2 always unsettles me."

"I have Julia Child as my chef. She's probably before your time. One of my most successful androids, although she babbles a bit too much and tends to sneak rich cream and real butter into the menu too often. All in all I—"

"Am I going to be able to control the Jake Troop android? At dinner he seemed pretty independent."

"There is a key phrase I've implanted in his brain," explained the robotics doctor. "When you say it and then follow it with an order or command, Jake-2 must obey. All of my mechanisms are structured this way nowadays. We had, in times past, some unfortunate accidents with the—"

Bang! Bang! Blam!

Shots had sounded downstairs. Also the breaking of glass.

Then feet running on the stairs. "It's nothing, it's okay." Lana dashed into the lab. "Jake-2 had a little shooting episode is all."

"Episode?" said Andy. "Who'd he shoot?"

The lovely Oriental girl shook her head. "No one, Andy. He shot the telly." She had changed from her warmup suit to a very sparse black dress. There was still no evidence of lingerie. "No need to fret."

Mackinson fingered the mole on his cheek. "Perhaps a few more modifications will be necessary before we release him to your custody, Mr. Stoker."

"Why did he shoot the TV?"

"There were some Indians on it," said the girl. "A newscast about the silly rain dance Sunshine McBernie staged this afternoon."

"Not so silly, we got two minutes of rain."

"That, dear Andy, was due to Nosmo Ifkovic using his cloud rockets this morning."

"Enough debating." Andy turned to the doctor. "Why's he do goofy things like this?"

"In order to make absolutely certain Jake-2 would be completely and thoroughly convincing," said Dr. Mackinson while moving for the door Lana stood in. "I pumped every single motion picture Jake Troop ever made into his brain."

"There is the possibility," amplified the lovely Lana, "the earlier films, which are highly jingoistic in regard to the relationships between the U. S. Cavalry and the Amerinds, have pushed Jake-2's mind a shade of kilter."

"No big thing," smiled Mackinson. "We can remedy it with a few flicks of the wrist."

"Unless he shoots you before you get a chance," said Andy.

———————◆———————

"They don't mind."

"I can just as well sit over on—"

"Nonsense. That's not cozy." Lana grabbed hold of one of the Dead End Kids androids by its scruffy armpits, yanked it off the low divan and dumped it to the floor. "Huntz Hall won't mind."

Huntz Hall rattled when he hit. "Hey, lady. Hey."

"Dumb squiff." Leo Gorcey spit on the rug.

"There isn't much," said Andy, "privacy around here."

"You get used to them." Lana was dressed now in a mid-thigh kimono of translucent neolon. Her position on the striped divan was fairly provocative. "Come settle beside me, Andy. On gloomy nights such as this, when the witching hour is fast approaching, I like to have someone nearby."

Andy accepted her invitation. "I would like to talk about Jake Troop . . . Jake-2 a bit more."

"Hardly a topic for snuggling up with." She slid one bare arm around his neck. "What I love to do when nestled snugly with someone I'm especially fond of is tell gruesome ghost stories. I find them a stimulating and exciting—"

"Thing is," persisted Andy, "this android of yours seems to me to be pretty volatile. This business earlier tonight, shooting the screen out of the televis—"

"Don't you know one single horrible tale, Andy?"

"After seven years in Hollywood?" He found himself straying from the major problem he wanted to discuss with the doctor's stunning associate. "See, Lana, I am going to have to escort this machine to Texas in a couple of weeks. Suppose he . . . it . . . suppose Jake-2 goes off on a rampage?"

"So?"

"What do you mean by 'so'?"

"Jake Troop is noted, even in the far corners of the world, for his wild and unconventional behavior. People have come to expect it of him," the girl expounded. "Therefore, and this is an important point to keep in mind about all of Dr. Mackinson's creations, Jake-2 has been constructed to duplicate those wild, uninhibited actions for which the actual Jake Troop is famous."

"The real Jake never shot up a television set," said Andy. "At least I don't think he did. Of course, Burns Prine and that gang keep a lot of things back from Stamms-Important, so I suppose even if he had I'd never—"

"Graveyards at midnight," interrupted Lana, stroking her fingertips into various crevices of his left ear. "They make good settings for ghost yarns. Tell me one, Andy."

"Dis guy must be some kinda pansy," observed Gabe Dell from his wicker armchair.

Leo Gorcey, after spitting deftly through closed teeth, said, "Naw, dis guy's jist chicken."

"Snarf snarf," laughed Huntz Hall, twisting his baseball cap into a new position on his head.

"There are," said Lana, "fewer of our mechanical men stored in my room. Would you like to continue our conversation there, Andy?"

"Whoops, my deah," snortled Leo Gorcey. "Dat's a proposition if I ever heard one."

"We all oughta go up to the skirt's room," suggested Billy Hallop.

"Snarf snarf," said Huntz Hall.

"Your room sounds like a good idea." Andy stood.

Lana stood, smoothing her scant kimono. "But you must promise to tell me a grisly ghost story."

"Sure, okay." He followed her across the midnight room and up a stairway.

"Save a little of dat stuff for me," called Huntz Hall.

"Hey, don't act so unsinfulized," cautioned Leo Gorcey.

Lana's upstairs bedroom was lit by a single floating globe or orangish light hanging above her four-poster bed.

Benjamin Franklin, spectacles askew, was slumped down in a far corner of the dim room. "It has been written," he said, "the mighty ocean only reaches to a fool's knees."

"That's an odd thing to come out of Ben Franklin," said Andy.

"He needs a few more adjustments. Somehow we programmed the wisdom of Confucius into him."

"You sure you haven't made any mistakes like that with Jake-2?"

"Do you notice him spouting any Eastern aphorisms?"

"No so far, no. But if I get down to Texas and he starts saying, 'Truly it is written,' and such, I'm going to be—"

"Forget Jake-2 for a while," advised Lana, slipping out of her flimsy robe. "Forget as well Jake Troop himself."

"Don't think I don't appreciate your friendliness, Lana." He averted his eyes from her unclothed body so as not to lose the thought he wanted to bring out. "I don't mind staying here a day or two in order to learn how to handle Jake-2. When I head back to Hollywood with him, though, I have to be absolutely sure he's in perfect working order. See, I'm going to have to smuggle him into my—"

"Come on." The girl grabbed his hand, shoved a foot into his ankle, and toppled him over onto the deep soft bed astride her. "Now make with a spooky story."

"Um, well, let's see. . . . Okay . . . it was midnight in the graveyard. Yeah, it was midnight in the graveyard and a wicked wind blew across the weed-high unkempt grounds, rattling the rusty iron gates of the ruined cemetery, rasping at the crumbling tombstones that huddled like forlorn derelics overlooked by the cruel passage of—"

"Ah I can feel a delicious chill spreading over me." Her arms hugged him.

"Mournful black clouds scudded across the murky moon and from the dark hilltop nearby came the eerie howls of some crazed beasts. The broken bell in the old decaying church tower tolled the dread hour of midnight as a lone figure . . ."

CHAPTER
SEVEN

"Androids," said a voice inside Andy's head. "Everybody's an android except me. I'm the last man alive on Earth, all the others are machines. There's a vast conspiracy to . . ."

He awakened. Very early sunlight was making its way into the girl's bedroom through the spaces beneath the drawn shades. Birds were starting to twitter out in the bushes against the old house.

"Early to bed and early to rise," remarked Ben Franklin, "makes a man healthy, wealthy, and wise."

"So I hear." He rubbed at his eyes, yawned, hunched his shoulders a few times.

Lana was asleep beside him. She slept in a very odd way, at least one he had never encountered before. Flat on her back, her arms straight down at her sides, with her fingers closed into fists. Her breathing was absolutely even, her breasts rising and falling in a completely predictable way.

She didn't toss or fret, make little noises, reach out a hand. "That's a very calm and mechanical way to . . ." Andy sat up. "Mechanical? Good lord!" He stared down at the beautiful Lana. "No, impossible. Mackinson isn't that good."

You couldn't make love to a robot and not know it. Oh maybe if you were a rube with little or no experience.

"But I've slept with literally . . ."

Still he'd never seen anyone sleep this way. Quite probably it was some form of Eastern mysticism. Do people in Tibet sleep like this? Stamms-Important had packaged a cable special on Tibetan Buddhism last season. Was there anything in that about how they slept?

"Listen to yourself. First you suspect a perfectly decent girl of being a machine, then you go making racial slurs about her."

Very cautiously he edged, shifting his backside in small

cautious hops, to the Ben Franklin side of the bed. Leaning toward the seated android, he whispered, "Say, Lana isn't . . . I mean, she's not . . . not a robot, is she?"

Ben Franklin adjusted his spectacles. "Of course not, young man."

"Good. I really didn't think she was, but you know, I had some strange dreams and I—"

"She's no more mechanical than I am."

Andy sighed out his breath. Obviously the damn androids were built to believe themselves human, to add to the deception. Therefore there was no way to be absolutely sure he hadn't spent the night with a highly believable machine.

"Well, what's so terrible about that?" he asked himself, ignoring the goosebumps that suddenly formed on his arms. "Think about the sex lives of some of our clients. Sleeping with a robot sounds pretty tame by comparison. Who's it hurt, after all? And, consider this, it's bound to be sanitary because you can't catch any kind of social disease off an android."

Or can you? Would Mackinson be so subtle? Could he build in something like that?

"Even if he could, he wouldn't want one of his customers to get the clap."

Andy scratched his head quietly while again studying the sleeping girl. She certainly was beautiful. So beautiful it made your bones ache to look at her. This absolutely couldn't be an android.

He reached out to touch her. Maybe this morning, in the clear light of day, the tactile—

"Good morning, Andy." Lana smiled, then opened her eyes. "How'd you know I adored being fondled awake?"

"Instinct, I guess."

Stretching up, she said, "I have a little alarm in my head, but this is better." She gave him a brief exuberant hug.

"In your head? Built in?"

"Ever since I was a little girl I've been able to tell myself when to wake up."

"Oh yeah, I see what you mean. You're speaking in metaphors."

"What else?" She rested her head against his bare chest. "You know what sort of stories I like to hear in the early-morning hours, Andy?"

"Regency romances?"

"Fairy tales. I love to pull the blankets up close to my chin while being told lighthearted tales of elves, gnomes, princesses, and the like," said Lana while bringing one filmy sheet up over her body. "Could you, do you think, oblige me?"

"You wouldn't settle for another ghost story? I have a couple good ones left over."

She laughed. "No, a new day with the sun pouring in is not the time for yawning graves and eldritch dread."

"Probably not. Okay, here's a quick one. Once upon a time on the edge of a deep dark forest there lived—"

Knock! Knock!

"Yes?" The Chinese girl called toward the door of her bedroom.

"We have, I fear, a bit of a problem," announced Dr. Mackinson from without.

"Is it Jake-2?" asked Andy.

"Ah, good morning, Mr. Stoker. I'm glad to see you and Lana have hit it off so well. Splendid girl, isn't she? Very bright."

Lana said, "What's the problem, doctor?"

"It is indeed Jake-2. I'm afraid he rode off from here not five minutes ago."

Andy leaped from bed and dived for the door. "In my car?"

"Oh no, no," said Dr. Mackinson. "He stole a horse."

CHAPTER

EIGHT

The crate was singing.

"Oh I am a lonely cowboy," it sang in a booze-blurred voice, "and I'm off on the Texas trail."

"Shut up in there," suggested Huck Levitz.

Andy and his friend were rising in one of the Stamms-Important Building's chrome and leatherette elevators.

Inside the large packing crate was the Jake Troop android.

"You have to use a special phrase to control him," said Andy. "*Ars longa, vita brevis*. Now quiet down, Jake-2."

"Oh when we get on the trail, boys, the dusty . . ." The song cut off, a little yodeling followed, and then there was silence inside the crate.

"He sang quite a lot coming down here in the station wagon I had to rent," said Andy. "At Fat Ed's Drive-in in Fresno he shot off one of his six-guns. I didn't even know he'd snuck the things inside there with—"

"Didn't that cause a stir?"

"Not in Fresno."

"Here we are."

The elevator hushed to a stop, its gleaming doors slid open. They had arrived at the thirtieth floor with the boxed android.

The floor was silent, filled mostly with darkness. A single light-strip lamp was glowing at the deserted reception desk.

Andy gripped the handle of the hand truck they'd put the crate on downstairs.

"Once down in Galveston," said Jake Troop's familiar voice, "a fella come up to me in the Longhorn Bar and called me a lop-eared mule skinner to my face. Well sir, I give him—"

"*Ars longa, vita brevis*. Hush up."

Levitz tugged at an ear. "Will you think I'm being overly critical if I mention I think he's a little quirky? I haven't met him as yet, but from lugging him up here from the car I'd—"

"He's not my invention." Andy was shoving the trucked crate across a vast stretch of faintly moonlit carpeting. "He's Dr. Mackinson's invention. I told Novella when I called her from up in Berkeley yesterday, as overtly as I could over a pixphone, I didn't have much faith in Jake-2."

"That's his name?"

"Yeah, to differentiate him from the real Jake."

Sprinting ahead of him, Levitz pushed open a door. "Poor Hoffning."

"Oh yeah, this is Hoffning's office. Is this where Novella wants Jake-2 stored? Won't Hoffning mind?"

"Hoffning is no more," explained Levitz as he flicked on the ceiling lights. "Killed himself day before yesterday."

Andy had wandered over to the window to watch the late-night Los Angeles streets. "Killed himself? How?"

"Jumped out that window. Amazing to me, since I've never known anybody who could get one of those open."

Andy backed away from the window. "Maybe we shouldn't kid about the poor guy's death."

"Why? Hoffning was a pain in the ass. If he hadn't jumped there was a whole cadre of people around here thinking about tossing him."

Shaking his head, Andy said, "Even so, even when a pain in the ass kills himself, it's sad. Know why he did it?"

"The ratings on *Geriatrics Hospital* came in that morning. Shortly thereafter Hoffning went out the window. I'd put in for his office, since it's six square feet larger than mine. I figure there may be a curse on it."

"Nobody says that to me and lives," said Jake-2 inside his box.

"*Ars longa, vita brevis* already!" Andy fisted his palm. "Boy, Huck, I am really not looking forward to traveling to Texas with this thing."

"Retire from show business then." Levitz sat in the swivel chair. "What an ugly family he had. Look at that wife, a face like the underside of a bathmat. And the daughters." He tipped over the tri-op photo.

"You're really not as heartless as you act. I think you mask your real feelings with this cynical stuff."

"Inside I'm an even bigger shit, or nerf, as Alicia Bramble would say. She's been phoning you, did I mention? Didn't you tell the girl what you were up to?"

"I'm going to tell the top-rated gossip in Hollywood I went to pick up a fake Jake Troop? I told her I was on a religious retreat."

"Alicia isn't the top-rated gossip in Hollywood, Harlo Glasspants is. Who told you she was?"

"Well, Alicia told me."

Levitz shook his head. "Who can one trust anymore? When a boy finds his one true love is conning him even within the confines of the—"

"You really don't think we should use this android, do you?"

"I have no opinions on the issue."

"Sure you do. Which is why you're needling me. Trying to goose me into taking a moral stand."

"I haven't goosed anyone into a moral stand for a long time." Levitz took a quick glance at the Hoffning family picture, then slapped it face down again.

"I have qualms myself." He took hold of the crate, began to worry the thing off the truck. "Up in Berkeley, after he stole the horse, I seriously—"

"He stole a horse? How do you go about doing that in Berkeley?"

"Dr. Mackinson's neighbors have three," explained Andy, shoving the packing crate across the floor. "Early in the morning Jake-2 broke out of the house, swiped a strawberry roan, and went riding for the center of town. He was intending to shoot Indians."

"Do they have any at the center of Berkeley?"

"This guy Sunshine McBernie, used to be Little Shoepolish in those old kid movies, brought some Indians into town for a rain dance. Do you think that stuff might actually work? There was about two minutes of—"

"Did your imitation Jake shoot any Indians?"

"No, he fell off his horse about five blocks from the doctor's place. See, Huck, there's another thing that doesn't bode well. After all, Jake Troop is a good horseman."

"Drunk or sober, right. How'd Mackinson explain that?"

"He claims this particular horse is used to a very tiny little old lady riding him. A big heavy robot spooked the animal, according to the good doctor."

"You believe him?"

"It's a very strange ménage he runs up there. What to believe and what not to believe, what's real and what isn't real . . . I'm not even certain Lana . . . well, no need to bring that up."

"Lana sounds like she might be a girl."

"She might," admitted Andy. "Now let's get this crate stashed over in the corner. I better get over to Alicia's to lie to her again about where I've been."

CHAPTER
NINE

"Well, he's leaking."

"Are you employing some polite euphemism? I wasn't aware our medical friend had constructed him so realistically that—"

"Actually he did, but this is oil," Andy whispered into the pixphone mike. "Some kind of bluish oil, the stuff is dripping out of his left ankle into his boot, Novella."

His boss's broad face nearly filled the hotel room phone screen. Her shaggy eyebrows went tilting toward each other. "Is he behaving properly otherwise?"

"Properly for Jake Troop, I guess," replied Andy. From the window of his suit in the Sheraton-Depletion Hotel he could see the dome of the brand-new Cowboy Heaven museum, which was built to resemble a gigantic Stetson hat. "He pinched the bellperson, took a swing at a blind teen-ager who asked for his voiceprint, threatened to shoot the guy who came to make the beds this morning. What I'm worried about, Novella, is this bluish oil dripping out of his ankle into—"

"It may well transpire, my lad, that no one in Texas will notice a little extra oil. One would presume they smell the stuff morning, noon, and night."

"Even so, the Sweetwater Kid was wrinkling his nose a little oddly when he dropped in to give us some PR bulletins this morning," said Andy. "Soon as I hang up with you I'm going to get in touch with Dr. Mackinson."

"Can that be a wise course to follow? Surrounded as you are by curious—"

"And there's another problem. Alicia Bramble is here in Drywell for the festivities. In fact, she's in this very hotel. You might have seen to it we were booked into a diff—"

"Stamms-Important people always reside at the best lodging in any given area. One can't prevent poor under-endowed Alicia for aspiring."

"She's wondering why I won't spend more time with her. Since we arrived last night I've been avoiding—"

"Surely she comprehends your first loyalty is to S-I?"

"She was looking at Jake-2, squinting actually, and—"

"Don't go calling him that in public, schmuck."

"Sorry, excuse it. Let me get hold of the doctor now, Novella."

"Very well, but use the utmost discretion. Else we . . . what is that unusual sound I note?"

"Oh that's him yodeling in the shower. I've grown used to it so I don't—"

"He takes showers?"

"As I told you, he does everything. As Mackinson explained it to me, the idea is—"

"Won't he rust?"

"Not supposed to, but then he's also not supposed to drip bluish oil."

"Call Mackinson. I shall contact you again ere nightfall."

"Okay, Novella. We've got the Cowboy Heaven opening banquet this evening, so I'm hoping Jake Troop is up to it."

"So hope we all." The screen went blank.

Andy took a few deep breaths. There was a fuzzy aching under his eyes and behind his ears. "Can you be allergic to Texas?" One more deep breath and he punched out the Berkeley, California, number.

Every time they went down to the lobby it seemed vaster and more crowded. This evening multitudes thronged the place, filled the Lucite chairs, milled on the sunburst carpeting, jostled around each of the plexipillars, shoved and elbowed to get away from the neoglass walls.

"We're worrying about his wart," a chubby woman said into Andy's ear.

"Where is it?" inquired the man, also chubby, with her.

"Well, doggone, buckaroo," said Jake-2 in his booming, husky voice. "Look who we got us here." He halted, grinned down at the couple who'd fought their way over to him.

Andy said, "The banquet, Jake. We really don't have time to—"

"Aw shucks, there's always time for my fans. How the heck you think I stayed on the top of the heap for so dang long? My fans kept me there. Ain't that right, Mr. and Mrs. Woolrich?"

Andy studied the plump couple as they pressed against him and his charge. "Oh yeah. I didn't recognize you folks. Sorry."

"You see, Rick, we do look younger," smiled the woman.

"Could be it's only our new hair coloring, Tess. What say, Mr. Stoker?"

"That's right, you didn't have green hair the last time we met."

"No, we were purple then," said Woolrich. "But enough about us. Where's your wart, Jake?"

Jake-2 touched his cheek. "You mean the one I used to have hereabouts?"

"No, it was up near your ear there." The green-haired woman pointed. "I hope it didn't turn out to be a malignant tumor. We'd sure hate to have to write up a malignant tumor in the newsletter."

"Oy," thought Andy. "Mackinson raves about 'warts and all' and he leaves off a wart."

"Shucks, buckaroos," chuckled Jake-2, "you can tell all them dedicated readers of *Jake's Troopers Fanzine* that the old Troop ain't got the big C, he's in the best shape he's been in since he was a little wee tad growing up in Merced, California."

"Modesto," said Woolrich, frowning. "You grew up in Modesto, Jake."

"Aw I was borned in Modesto, but I done a lot of my growing up in Merced," explained the cowboy mechanism. "By that I mean they had this first-class nookie palace in Merced that just simple outshone anything little old Modesto could offer. There was a Spanish girl in particular who done more for my education than any of them profs I had while I was playing football at—"

"Jake," put in Andy, "all your fans don't want to read about anything like that in their newsletter."

"On the contrary, Mr. Stoker," said Tess Woolrich. "This is exactly the kind of humanizing data we need. Makes the whole expensive trip here to Drywell worthwhile, doesn't it, Rick?"

"Right you are, Tess."

"Well sir," continued the android, "this Spanish girl couldn't have been no more than fifteen and they called her La Paloma. Never did learn her real name, but like that Kipling feller put it, I learned about women from her. Her real specialty was—"

"You'll excuse us, Mr. and Mrs. Woolrich." Andy tugged at the cowboy's arm. "Jake would stay here all night talking to his fans. That's the kind of guy he is, as I'm sure you know. We do, though, have to get across to the Cowboy Heaven museum for the banquet. Can't keep Governor Troff and all the other celebrity guests waiting."

"Aw I've knowed Herky Troff since he was a can rusher for a massage shop over in Beaumont. Sitting through a whole feed with that wall-eyed galoot will give a stone-deaf mule the heaves."

"Beautiful," said Mrs. Woolrich. "You speak just like you do in your films in real life, Jake."

Jake-2 shoved the brim of his cowboy hat up with a weathered thumb and winked at the chubby woman. "Tell you something else, ma'am. I ain't a actor at all. Nope, I'm just me. Plain old rough-edged Jake Troop, sixty-two years old and I ain't never been nothing on the screen 'cept myself."

"Sixty-five, aren't you, Jake?" said Woolrich.

"Let you nice folks in on something else. When you get up over sixty you like to chop a few years off. Leastways I—"

"Eek! Ouch!" A strikingly pretty blonde girl in a brief ivory-and-gold majorette costume had been passing behind Jake. After screaming, she ran slim fingers over her backside. "Sir, I don't fancy being tweeked on the . . . Oh my god, it's Jake Troop!"

Jake-2 turned, tipped his hat, and grinned at her. "One thing I can't resist, miss, is a well-wrought fanny."

"Well . . . gosh . . . usually I resent having my . . . but, my god, you're Jake Troop!"

Jake-2 leaned toward the young girl. "I'm staying in Suite 27B, which ain't widely known. Maybe sometime around midnight or thereabouts you—"

"Good night, all." Andy gave an enormous tug on the android's arm and managed to lead him away. When he had him approaching an exit door he said, "You're not to do things like that."

"Don't fret so much, buckaroo," advised Jake-2. "If I didn't grab a few buttocks now and then folks might get the notion (a) I ain't Jake Troop or (b) Jake's really getting old and feeble." Unlike some of Mackinson's androids, Jake-2 was fully aware he was an imitation. "Now, we don't want neither of them idears to get floating around. Ain't that so?"

"Yeah, yeah. But you're not going to seduce some little girl who twirls a baton simply to—"

"Aw there ain't no such thing as seducing, pard. I bedded down a heck of a lot of ladies in my time, and my time ain't up yet, and I never did meet one single one who didn't want—"

"Be that as it may, I'm not going to let some unspoiled Texas child get screwed by a machine. So watch it."

"Haw haw. That kid was about as innocent as La Paloma back in Merced."

"Also take it easy with the bio stuff."

"Ever word is gospel true, buckaroo."

"I know, I've reviewed Jake's life pretty thoroughly. Things like his whorehouse adventures I'd just as soon the general public didn't—"

"Shucks, pard, for a feller in the talent biz you sure now got some old-fangled idears. I know dang well my box-office rating goes up ever time they find out I been diddling some new—"

"Jake, how could you do it? How?" A lean old man in a rumpled tweed suit caught hold of the android's shoulder as they stepped out onto the people-filled street. "How could you, Jake?"

Andy recognized the man. "Jim, Jake doesn't make those decisions. On this—"

"Shut up, punk," said James Denver Fargo, the veteran Western novelist and screenwriter. "I'm talking to Jake Troop, to my lifelong friend. Jake, you son-of-a-bitch, how come I'm not scripting *Saddle Tramp?*"

"Like the youngster told you, Jimmy boy," said the android, putting a hand on the old man's bent back. "They don't let me make them decisions no more."

"Bullshit," said Fargo, his bloodshot eyes narrowing. "You call all the shots still."

"No more, Jimmy. Getting a picture financed now, you got to kiss a whole lot of new and unexpected fannies. Arab fannies," Jake told the swaying old writer. "These

Arabs, Jimmy, they don't care nothing for sentiment. Get us the hottest writers in town else we don't bankroll you. That's the way the game gets played."

"Gumbert and Snett? They're the hottest writers in Hollywood? Gumbert and Snett, a couple of punks who neither one of them is even thirty."

"They won an Oscar last year."

"For a musical about incest. They don't even know which end of the horse the crap comes out of. Did those punks ever write anything like *Gunfight at Battle Mountain, Last Stage to Indian Springs, Gunfight at Eureka, Gunfight at Oak Creek, Last Stage to Del Norte, Gunfight at Pagosa Springs, Last Stage to Durango, Gunfight at—*"

"Jimmy, you got a great list of credits. And you and me, you old waddie, made some darn fine films together. But shucks, I'm an old man myself and if I—"

"I get it, Jake. You're putting me out to pasture. I see the handwriting on the wall. They invite me down here to honor me for my contribution to the Western film and I can't even get—"

"Mr. Fargo, I have to get Jake over to that banquet," said Andy. "Why don't you call me when we're back in L.A.? I'm sure I can get you some TV work to—"

"Stuff it, punk." Fargo spun, went stumbling away from them down the night street.

"One good thing about being a robot, buckaroo, is you never get old." Jake-2 put an arm around Andy's shoulders. "Let's get us to that there banquet. I need some cheering up."

CHAPTER

TEN

Drip!
  Drip!
  Drip!
Trying to give the impression he was listening atten-
tively to the speaker at the lectern to the right of their

table, Andy very carefully lifted a corner of the stiff white tablecloth.

There was a bluish splotch on Jake-2's left knee. As Andy furtively watched, a bubble of oil formed in the spot's center and then fell. It hit the cowboy's ornate boot, like several drops before it apparently, then rolled thickly to the banquet-room floor.

"Did you drop one of your spareribs, buckaroo?" inquired Jake-2 out of the corner of his mouth.

"You've sprung," he informed the mechanical man in a hushed voice, "another leak."

"Aw I knew that. Don't fret none."

Andy let the tablecloth fall. He rested his fingertips on a biscuit, watching T. Tex Harbler addressing the five hundred people in the banquet hall of Cowboy Heaven.

The venerable singing-cowboy actor wiped a tear from his eye. ". . . in all them many motion pictures," T. Tex was saying, "there weren't not one moment of senseless violence, nor was there no perverse sex. No, my friends, for in those great and bygone days, days which this marvelous new museum is dedicated to honoring, we had no use for perverse sex and senseless . . ."

How was Jake-2 going to deliver his speech while spouting oil? According to the program the Sweetwater Kid had slipped them, Jake Troop was scheduled to follow T. Tex. The lectern would hide his legs from most of the audience, but he was bound to drip while walking from the head table to the microphone. So how to account for that?

Andy scanned their table. There was a cruet of salad oil sitting three places over, directly in front of Rance Keane. The bastard who used to cohabit with Alicia Bramble. He hated to ask somebody like that to pass the salad oil.

"Is there something you need?" asked the statuesque brunette on his left. It was Betti Sue Boonfarm, the nation's leading country-and-western singer.

"Salad oil."

Betti Sue blinked. "You ate all your salad long since," she whispered.

"I always take a teaspoonful of oil after each meal. For my digestion."

"Oh really? I never heard tell of—"

"Hush up, girl." The stunted old man next to Betti Sue nudged her.

"Did you know, Mort, that salad oil—"

"Hush," repeated her gnomish husband. "You're among quality folks now, you got to stop acting so country."

"Did you meet my husband earlier?" the large girl asked Andy. "He's Mort Boonfarm, the noted oil tycoon."

"Pleased to meet you. Could you pass the salad oil?"

"Why the hell for?"

"It helps his digestion, Mort. Don't be such a grouch."

". . . not one bare pink thigh ever marred a T. Tex Harbler Western motion picture. Not one curvaceous breast ever dared angle in . . ."

Old man Boonfarm's nose wrinkled. "Speaking of oil," he said, "I surely smell it."

"There's a whole jug of it almost smack in front of you, Mort."

"Not that kind of oil, girl. I mean *oil* oil." He lifted the tablecloth. "You don't suppose those idiots built this museum over valuable oil land?"

"Mort's got a nose for oil," Betti Sue explained in a low voice. "That's how he found so many wells and became a billionaire. Smelled them."

Boonfarm was upright again. "I'll have to talk to the Cowboy Heaven folks later. Might be they'll let me sink a few—"

"You ain't going to drill big holes in this new shrine, Mort."

"Salad oil," whispered Andy to the girl singer.

"Pass the salad oil, Mort."

One of Boonfarm's roughhewn hands grabbed the cruet. "Here. Now hush up."

"Here." Betti Sue handed it over to Andy.

"Thanks." He placed the cruet beside his plate.

After a few more seconds the girl asked, "Ain't you going to take it?"

"Take what?"

"The teaspoonful of salad oil."

"Oh yeah, to be sure. I got enthralled in T. Tex's speech and nearly forgot." He took up a spoon and filled it with oil.

Just as he thrust the spoon between his lips he had the sensation someone was staring at him. Despite the subdued lighting of the enormous banquet hall Andy saw two frosty blue eyes glaring at him with surprising clarity. The eyes belonged to Alicia Bramble, who was scowling at him from three tables away.

"Why do you hate me?" she mouthed.

"I don't," he pantomimed once he got the spoon out of his mouth.

"You're avoiding me."

"But I'm not."

"Are those lip exercises part of the digestion business?" asked Betti Sue.

"Yes, yes, that's right." Andy broke eye contact with the golden-haired gossip. "Few people realize that the lip muscles connect directly with the colon."

"I didn't realize that."

"Few people do."

Wiping away another tear, T. Tex Harbler said, "It now gives me a great pleasure, folks, to introduce to you another great cowboy actor. I always think of him as a young feller, but I noticed tonight he's got a little touch of snow on the roof. Been a pal of mine for an awful lot of years . . . Jake Troop."

Jake-2, grinning, stood up.

"Oops." Andy slapped the oil cruet, causing it to flip off the banquet table and hit against the android's leg. "Gee, sorry, Jake. Looks like I spilled oil all over you," he said in a loud voice.

"Had a lot worse dumped on me in my day, buckaroo," said the big cowboy with a chuckle.

The banquet crowd echoed the chuckle.

Jake-2 made his way to the lectern, and Andy bent to retrieve the fallen cruet. When he looked out at the audience again he became aware of another pair of eyes scrutinizing him.

A slender red-haired girl was watching him from a table farther away than the gossip's. She was pretty, but then most of the women Andy got involved with were that. This girl had some extra quality, though, something he couldn't quite place. It made her especially attractive to him.

"Honesty," he realized all at once. "She radiates honesty." With a shake of his head he looked away from her.

"Well sir, when I was growing up in Merced, California," Jake began, "I made myself a sort of a promise. That promise was that I'd grow up to be as good and decent a man as my boyhood idol, T. Tex Harbler, and, you know, I think I kept . . ."

CHAPTER
ELEVEN

"No doubt the major film notable to grace Drywell for this event is Jake Troop," the television set said. "Crowds of sightseers who've been flocking into our town for the gala opening of the Cowboy Heaven museum seem almost unanimous in their feelings that the Oscar-winning cowboy veteran is the man who—"

"This humping bed is harder than a faro dealer's heart," complained Jake-2.

"Be glad you don't sleep in a crate." Andy was slumped in a wing chair in the cowboy android's bedroom. It was a few minutes past eleven at night. He turned the set off with the control box in his hand.

"Them festivities over to the museum was just getting interesting when you drug me off, buckaroo. Don't see why we had to come home." Jake-2 was stretched out on an oval bed, hands behind his head, Stetson tilted far forward.

"We had to repair that oil spill on your knee."

"Aw that didn't interfere none with my funning," said Jake-2. "Sides, lots of them folks at the banquet got a real kick out of seeing me. Ain't that what they just now said on the tube?"

"You're not really Jake Troop," Andy reminded him. "You're a machine, and if you go dribbling much more oil people will commence realizing it. We're not here in Drywell so you can have fun, we're here so everybody will be deluded into believing Jake Troop is in perfect health."

"Don't seem quite honest," observed Jake. "Now, when I was marshal of Dodge City I always made—"

"Jake Troop was never a marshal anyplace. Don't start getting your movie roles mixed up with real life."

"Shucks, my movies and my life are all rolled into one. Like I was telling them Woolrich folks down to the lobby tonight, pard, I ain't never portrayed nothing on that silver screen 'cept my own—"

"Okay, it's bedtime for you. I've got to go have a drink with Alicia Bramble over at a place called the Cattleman's Rest. She's starting to suspect things aren't—"

"Son, I sure wouldn't bust my gut over a girl with such small chest equipment," drawled Jake-2.

"It's not her chest I'm concerned about at the moment. It's the fact she can inform millions of people you are a fake."

"I ain't no fake. I'm a genuine one-of-a-kind cowpoke. Honest as the—"

"*Ars longa, vita brevis.*" Andy left his chair. "You'll now go to sleep and awaken at eight in the morning."

"Sure, I can do that. I got a little alarm clock in my headbone."

"Which reminds me. You know Lana Woo . . . never mind. Go to sleep."

In ten seconds the android was producing highly believable snores.

◀━━━━●━━━━▶

A wind had risen, hot and dry. It brushed at Andy as he hurried, a shade reluctantly, toward his rendezvous with Alicia. The bar was only a few blocks from the hotel and he passed the Cowboy Heaven hat-shaped museum while walking on his way there.

The festivities were continuing inside. Twangy electric music flowed out, causing some of the sightseers outside to bounce in tempo. The bright-lit display windows featured wax figures of William S. Hart, Hoot Gibson, and Tom Mix engaged in a dull-looking saloon brawl with a flock of owlhoots. None of the figures was anywhere near as convincing as Jake-2. With a quick glance at them, Andy continued on.

Next to the museum was a multilevel parking garage. From up on the open second or third level came the faint sound of a girl crying out. Then a crackling sound.

Andy slowed. "What's going on up there?"

One more cry prompted him to go jogging up an entry ramp.

"I sure don't mean you no harm, missy. This here's how we pay attention to a cute little trick back home whereat I come from."

Andy used the voice as a guide. It was coming from the third level of the Cowboy Heaven garage.

The voice belonged to a broad man of fifty. Dressed all in black cowboy attire, including black boots and a black ten-gallon hat, he held a bull whip in his gloved right hand. Andy had seen him earlier down at the banquet, though the man hadn't been carrying the whip then. He was Whipper Wentworth, the cowboy actor who'd made a few quickies decades ago, back in the 1950s some time.

The girl Andy also recognized. It was the red-haired girl with the honest aura. There was a rip up the side of her short lycra skirt, one sleeve of her dress had been torn off.

"This is a private confab, bud," Whipper informed him.

Ignoring the cowboy, Andy crossed to the girl. "What's going on?"

"He followed me out of the banquet when I left to get my car. You're Andy Stoker, aren't you?"

"Yeah, I am. What's he up to?"

"Wants me to go to bed with him, I imagine. The whip stunts are to impress me, and to keep me from running off."

"Is that what tore your clothes?"

"Yes, he—"

Crack!

The tongue of the long whip curled around Andy's ankle, causing a jagged pain. Without much thought he bent and took hold of the whip. He yanked and Whipper Wentworth fell over before letting go of the handle.

Andy had seen that done in several old Jake Troop films, though he realized now it had only worked in this instance because Whipper was considerably drunk.

"You hadn't ought to knock down a Western great," complained the actor from a flat-out position.

Andy threw the whip over the edge of the low wall. "You leave her alone from now on," he said evenly.

"Nobody talks to Whipper Wentworth that way."

"Get out of here! Right now! Or I'll toss you after your bleeping whip!"

"Only being friendly, I was." Wentworth scrambled to his feet. "Down home whip tricks break the ice real good."

"Maybe you better get down home fairly quick," suggested Andy.

Dusting his black hat off very swiftly, Wentworth went stumbling away.

"I appreciate your help, Mr. Stoker."

Andy was watching the retreating black-clad cowboy and trying to get his breathing to level out to normal. "I usually am not this aggressive."

"Well, you did a very nice job of helping me out of a pretty odd situation," the red-haired girl told him. "I don't think I've ever been molested by a man with a whip before."

"I ought to see that you get home safely."

"That would be nice. I'm staying out on the edge of town at the HoJo-Corral. You can drive over there with me in my car and then get a cab back to the Sheraton-Depletion. Or is that too much trouble?"

"No, no trouble. How'd you know where I was staying?"

"I'm Frankie Bentin." She held out her hand. "I work for Four Corners-Mutual Insurance."

While shaking her hand he realized who she must be. "You're an investigator for the company that's insuring the *Saddle Tramp* production. I remember your name now."

"Yes, that's right. We've probably corresponded in the past. I work out of FCM's San Francisco office."

"What brings you to Texas?"

"Jake Troop," she said. "I've been hearing some rumors about him. I have to get a good look at him for myself."

"A good look," Andy repeated.

"I'm sure you can arrange that."

"Sure." Andy nodded. "Oh sure."

CHAPTER
TWELVE

"Yeah, it's an item."

"Nerf yourself."

"Cowboy great goes berserk with bull whip. That's an item if I ever heard one."

"Sloop yourself."

Andy paused, attempting to relax in the pseudocowhide booth of the crowded and murky cocktail lounge. "Well, anyway, that's why I'm a little late."

"A little? Fifty-three nerfing minutes is 'a little' to you?" Grim-faced, the lovely Alicia Bramble sat with arms folded beneath her small breasts. "Even Abou Ben Adam at Warners-Mecca Films never keeps me cooling my fricky for fifty-three harping minutes."

"Whipper Wentworth, the cowboy great, went berserk with his famous bull whip. I couldn't very well stand by watching him flail—"

"Whipper Wentworth hasn't been a flapping cowboy great since eons ago. The last time I even mentioned Whipper Wentworth was for a Where are they now? seg on my show over two years back. At the time he was a street-corner preacher for the Aquatic Pentacostal Church down in Anaheim somewhere. Do you honestly think I'd smerk up my show with an item about a—"

"Be that as it may, Alicia, you now have the reason for my arriving late. How are you otherwise?"

"Do you have any idea how many of these slooping has-been cowboys tried to pick me up while you were off rescuing some slatternly bimbo from—"

"She wasn't slatternly at all, Alicia. She was quite—"

"A dozen or more. Even that senile old foop T. Tex Harbler came over to grope at my wimpies. Can you imagine his nerfing audacity? He was in films in the thirties, eons ago. There's the chief trouble with these nostalgic events—they bring out every washout in the world."

"I saw a neobronze statue of T. Tex in the museum. That must prove he's an entity."

"I haven't seen his nerfing statue, but I bet it's got one hand poised in the act of unzipping the fly," said the beautiful golden-haired gossip. "What are you keeping from me?"

"Hum?"

"Even before you stood me up tonight, Andy, you were acting extremely bizarre." She unfolded her arms, spread her hands wide. "I tell you it's a slooping problem being fond, truly fond of someone as sneaky as you. When I was amorously involved with Rance Keane I—"

"What did you think of his speech at the banquet? Not too subtle, shooting off his guns like that."

"Don't try to distract me. There's something about Jake Troop. Something you don't want me to find out about."

"Alicia, we have a rule about allowing show business to intrude into our—"

"What's wrong? I can sense it. I rose from my humble beginnings to become the top-rated gossip in the world because I have an unfailing sense about things like this. If somebody's got something dirty buried, I know it." She tapped her chest.

"By the way, I heard the other day it's Harlo Glass-pants who is actually the top-rated gossip in—"

"A nerfing lie! That diminutive frick couldn't gossip his way out of a . . . ah no. No you don't, Andy. Let's return to the topic of Jake Troop and what it is about him you're attempting to conceal from me. Me, to quote you, 'the only human you ever cared deeply and truly about.'"

"Did I say that? Doesn't sound like my style of exposition. Not that the basic sentiments expressed—"

"Back to Jake Troop. What is wrong with him? Why, for instance, is he not here tonight celebrating with all his cowpoke cronies?"

"Well, Alicia," began Andy slowly, "Jake is back at the hotel. Now, I can honestly tell you that the guy in that hotel room is in absolutely great shape. Thing is, he's making a serious effort to reform. Don't scoff. Jake Troop is going over the script for *Saddle—*"

Kafloppo!

A Japanese cowboy had come sailing by their booth, arms flapping, black-booted feet kicking, to land on his backside on the sawdusted floor.

Alicia glanced down at him. "Is he worth an item?" She rubbed at her lovely chin.

"Who is he?"

"Don't you recognize Tomo Taipuraita? He's the hottest actor in Japan right now. They're absolutely gaga over Westerns over there again and Tomo's the king of the cowboys."

The medium-sized actor was shaking his head, eyes not quite in focus. He felt around for his sombrero.

"Smile when you say that to me, you little brown devil!" shouted someone at the far end of the bar. "Next time I'll do a lot more than punch you."

"Oops." Andy stood, stared, sat, smiled unevenly at the girl.

"Up to his old tricks."

"Now that we've taken care of that pesky runt, it's drinks for one and all," roared Jake-2.

"Guess he . . . guess he had enough script for one night . . . ventured out for a nightcap."

"This is definitely an item. Cowboy great breaks training to slug box-office fave from Land of Rising Sun. Good, not bad."

"Wait now, Alicia, it won't sound . . ." Why not, though? Sure, if she tells her millions of viewers Jake Troop was in a saloon brawl in Texas, it'll kill the rumors about his being sickly. "That's right, I promised not to interfere with your work. Excuse me a minute, though, I'd best talk to Jake."

"Do. I'll be phrasing the item in my head. I've got a typewriter in there."

"You do?" He frowned down at her as he rose. "Oh yeah, a metaphor. See you soon." He slid away, pushed around T. Tex Harbler, Squinty Truid, the Hootowl Kid, and Betti Sue Boonfarm.

"You're looking well, except a little pale," observed the singer as he eased by her.

"Not getting enough salad oil probably." He dived, pivoted, and reached the android's side. "Well, hello, Jake. Had enough of the old script for one night, eh?"

"Had enough of that little slant." Jake-2's fist circled a stein of ale.

"I instructed you," said Andy close to the mechanism's ear, "to remain in bed. You're not supposed to be able to overcome my orders."

"Usually I can't," admitted Jake-2. "I figure as how it was the Sweetwater Kid's dropping in which jiggled my gears."

"Don't talk about gears so loud," said Andy. "What do you mean the Sweetwater Kid dropped in?"

"Come by to visit, talk up old times. Being the Sweetwater Kid, a-course, he come in through the window."

"Window? We're on the twenty-seventh floor."

"Aw that Kid's a tricky feller. Many's the time I seen him come boots-first through a pane of glass you'd think no human critter could enter by way of. Nice old guy, too. In a way, I'm sorry I cold-cocked him."

"Whoa. You knocked the Sweetwater Kid out?"

"We got to jawing, cutting up touches 'bout the Golden Age of horse operas and one thing led to another and afore you know it he's throwing punches. The Kid's game but his footwork is far from perfect anymore. Can't expect your head to stay clear if you're all the time jumping through—"

"What happened to him?"

"Far as I know he's still flat on his butt on the floor of our suite, buckaroo. When I deck 'em they stay decked."

"You can't do that to the PR director of the whole damn Cowboy Heaven complex."

"Already done it. I'm a dang good dirty fighter."

"Come along, we have to revive him."

"I only just begun to celebrate, buckaroo."

"Nevertheless. *Ars longa, vita brevis.*"

"Okay, have it your way." Jake-2 lifted his Stetson, waved it in the smoky air, and gave a whoop. "See you all later on. Whenever you're out Buckaroo Ranch way, drop in. Night, folks."

Andy caught Alicia's attention. "Back in a while."

"Nerf you," she mouthed in reply.

CHAPTER

THIRTEEN

"How come you're walking funny, buckaroo?"

"Got a stiff shoulder," replied Andy as he and the android crossed the airport terminal toward the Wildcatter Cocktail Lounge. "Sleeping in a suite lacking window panes did it. How'd you guys manage to break so many?"

"Well sir, it could be that after the Sweetwater Kid

come crashing in to visit me last night I maybe said as
how sure it was a crackerjack way to drop in. Which
might of inspired him to go out and come in again via another window. The Kid always has been a mite show-
offy."

"Well, at least you didn't permanently disable him."

"The dang hotel sawbones already told you the Kid'll
be up and around in no time."

"Hope he doesn't sue us."

"Ain't that what we need, buckaroo? An old coot with a
bum ticker couldn't cold-cock a burly stuntman. So it
seems to me the more brawls I get into, the better it is for
the cause."

"Maybe so, except Novella gets very antsy over law-
suits. That Taipuraita guy is going to take legal action,
claiming you permanently damaged his gun hand."

"That's a corker," chuckled Jake-2. "He ain't got
enough savvy to pull a six-shooter out of his holster, let
alone shoot off the thing."

At the wide black door of the airport bar Andy halted.
"Be very careful with this girl we're going to meet," he
warned his charge. "She's got doubts about Jake Troop's
health, and if the Four Corners-Mutual people have
doubts, we could all be in trouble."

"Shucks, you don't have to tell Jake Troop how to act
around a girl." He pushed the door open.

Only a few people were in the blue-lit afternoon cocktail lounge. But there was Frankie, wearing trousers and a

crisp blouse, her long red hair tied back with a twist of ribbon. She sat alone at a round black table.

"Here's Jake Troop, just as I promised last night." Andy's voice didn't sound quite right to him. Something about this particular girl threw him off kilter. "Frankie Bentin, Jake Troop."

"This is a doggone pleasure, miss." Jake-2 swept off his Stetson, bowed, and clicked his boots together. He took the chair nearest the girl, gave her a Jake Troop grin. "I can see why this waddie was so all-fired anxious to keep this here appointment with you before we took off for home."

Andy seated himself. "Nobody else's been bothering you?"

"No. No whips or anything." She smiled at him.

"Glory be, it's Jake Troop!" Their waitress, who wore a yellow construction-worker helmet with her black bikini, had reached their table. "It is, isn't it?"

"Yep, it sure as heck is." Jake-2 grinned at her.

"Glory be. I been seeing you in the movies since I was nothing but a little bitty girl child."

"Well sir, that makes me right happy." Jake-2 nodded slowly. "Cause I don't make movie pictures simple for the money, though I got to admit I like the stuff. Nope, I also make the countless epics of the Old West 'cause I want to entertain folks. Especially pretty little button-nose folks like yourself. Fact of it is, if I weren't heading for the Buckaroo Ranch out in California in a matter of hours I'd—"

"We better order, Jake," cut in Andy. "What are you drinking, Miss Bentin?"

"I'm fine with this ginger ale."

"I'll have a plain scotch. You, Jake?"

"I bet you this little button-nose girl knows what I drink."

"Ale," answered the waitress.

"See, buckaroo, that there's a real nice part 'bout being a famous person. People knows all about you, what you like." He administered a friendly pat to the girl's buttocks. "You better run fetch them drinks, honey, seeing as my pard here is the anxious kind."

"Yes, Mr. Troop. Glory be."

"I can't help liking people," Jake-2 confided in Frankie. "Special if they is pretty girls."

"How are you feeling, Mr. Troop?" she asked.

He laughed. "Get right to it, huh? Doggone, I like a direct woman. With that pretty little button-nose waitress, with her you'd have to diddle and daddle before you ever got things out in the open. Not so with you, Frankie. Cards on the table. Darned if I don't like that a whole lot."

"So how's your health?"

"How do I look?" He stretched his arms wide, flexed his muscles.

"I have to say," she said, mostly to Andy, "you look exceptionally fit, Mr. Troop."

"Whyn't you call me Jake? Most folks do," invited the android. "Let me tell you, Frankie, I ain't never been in better condition. That's the Bible truth. Why, only last night . . . Aw I guess Andy don't want we should talk about that."

"I've already heard about the brawl," said the red-haired insurance investigator.

"Which one?" asked Jake-2.

"Here's your ale, Mr. Troop. I hope you enjoy it."

"I'm sure I will, miss."

The hard-hatted girl placed Andy's drink before him and scampered away.

"Were you in more than one brawl, Jake?" Frankie asked, sipping at her ginger ale.

"Well, I don't rightly know if you'd call any of them little bitty encounters brawls. I tangled with the Sweetwater Kid up to the hotel room and later I got into a sort of fracas with a Jap. Mean to say, though, picking up one old worn-out giant stuntman and decking him . . . or tossing a midgety Nip the length of a room . . . that's no brawl in either case. Not like the ones we used to have in the old days on location with John Ford."

"When you threw Mr. Taipuraita across the Cattleman's Rest last evening," inquired Frankie, "did you experience any after-effects? Pains across the chest, palpitations, soreness in your arms?"

Jake-2 laughed, slapped at his knee. "I didn't have me no heart attack, if that's what you're wanting to know."

"You feel well this afternoon?"

"I honestly do believe, Frankie, I could whup a whole mess of wildcats and not get one single palpitation." He laughed some more, then drank a good percentage of his ale.

Frankie looked directly at Andy. "Thank you for letting me get together with you," she said, smiling at him. "And thanks again for last night. I'm sure I'll see you again."

"I'd like that, yeah."

The girl stood up. "I'll leave you now. We'll probably meet soon, on the *Saddle Tramp* location if not before."

Andy got to his feet. "You'll be at the location filming?"

"Yes, I will."

"Oh well . . ." Andy said.

She smiled once more and left.

Andy was filled with mixed feelings.

CHAPTER
FOURTEEN

"That's dreadful," said Huck Levitz' wife, Naomi. A thin, dark-haired girl, she stood at the redwood railing of their wide sundeck watching part of Higado Canyon burn away far below. "Look at those expensive homes burning up."

"Shouldn't you," asked Andy, "be thinking of evacuating?"

"No, the fire won't get this high. Never does." The twenty-seven-year-old woman's hands were lightly dusted with whole-wheat flour. "If Southern California had a sensible water policy things like that wouldn't happen. . . . Oh there goes Roscoe Buford's house. Did you see him in *Knee Jerk?* Well, I'd better get back to my bread. Huck should be off the pix in a minute."

"Fine." Andy shifted in his lycra slingchair.

Black smoke was furling up through the late afternoon, climbing straight through the thin blue. You could see the flames eating away tiny house after tiny house, turning trees black, wiping out dry lawns. None of the sound of the canyon fire reached this high. Everything burned away in silence, and the black, acrid smell hadn't reached here yet.

"What am I going to do with Twitchy Ploog?" Huck returned to the sundeck. "Looks like a bad fire this time."

"What's Twitchy want?"

"A part in *Airport '86*. I'm trying to get Ehrhardt to let her read for the part of the leprous Brazilian commando, but he says her wimpies are too small." Turning his back on the distant fire, Levitz sat in a plexirocker. "All these years in the business and I'm still embarrassed when I have to tell a client her wimpies are too small."

"Twitchy's won two Oscars."

"Yeah, but not for wimpies. You can't prod Ehrhardt

with rational reasoning anyway. Got anybody on your client list who can do the leprous Brazilian commando?"

Andy thought. "Maybe Hazel Werf."

"Too big."

"How about Nell Brinkley? I could send her over to Ehrhardt."

His friend shut his eyes for a few seconds. "Yeah, I visualized Nell's bosom. It might do. Give him a call tomorrow, tell him she's dying to read for him. Meantime I'll find something else for Twitchy."

"Okay, I'll do that."

"You didn't come over to talk bosoms. How was Texas?"

"Well, something . . . strange happened."

"Didn't the android work?"

"He functioned okay. Except for a slight tendency to leak oil."

"You got him back in his crate at the office all right?"

"Last night, under cover of darkness. He yodeled a bit, then quieted down," said Andy as he cracked his knuckles. "Jake-2 is safely repacked and locked in Hoffning's office."

"Think you'll need him again?"

"I'm hoping not. According to Burns Prine, Jake is—"

"You're talking about Jake-1 now?"

"Yeah, the real Jake Troop will be in sufficient good health to venture down to Inferno, New Mexico, next month to begin shooting *Saddle Tramp*. Dr. Faustus concurs."

"Dr. Faustus?" Levitz laughed. "Don't tell me—"

"No jokes about his name. Now about what happened in—"

"Huck, another one." Naomi reappeared on the deck with an enormous lump of dough clutched in her two hands.

"Excuse me, Andy." He trotted inside to the pixphone.

"It's Stooge McAlpin," said Naomi, kneading while she spoke. "Do you remember him? The first time I ever had sexual congress with Huck we played—"

"He's a waiter now. Why is he—"

"Wants to make a comeback. He thinks he'd be perfect for the captain in *Ship of Fools '87*."

"I never saw a ship captain with sequins implanted."

"Have you looked at the script? This captain is supposed to be an ex-rock star who turned to the sea as a calling. Could just be the exact part Stooge needs." She punched the big ball of dough a few times. "I hope you'll excuse my excessive feminine role-playing, but I'd better return to the kitchen."

"Sure."

Not so much smoke from down below. Possibly they were starting to get it under control. Unconsciously Andy tucked his feet in, as though pulling them back from potential flames.

"He might work out," Levitz said.

"Stooge?"

"The guy's personable. You saw that the other day at Mock's. Yeah, he could work out. I'll phone Gomez-

Gomez tonight at his hideaway down in Baja. He only talks business from midnight to 1 A.M. Stooge McAlpin as the captain, not bad."

"Better for a steward."

"Give the poor bastard a chance to escape from his menial status."

"About Texas," said Andy.

"Met a girl?"

"Well, yes."

"I thought Alicia was down in Drywell for that opening."

"She was. The thing is, Huck, I didn't want to spend much time with Alicia because—"

"Huck. Again."

"Excuse me." He left the sundeck.

"All our weekends are like this," confided the thin Naomi. She didn't have the ball of whole-wheat dough this time.

"Who wants him now?"

"Oh it's Cleveland Jazzbo Birmingham Brown," answered Naomi. "Alicia's little hatchet man. Did you know his real name is Nafaka Kama Ngano? He decided to change it to something more in keeping with his American traditions. I never trust him."

"He is a bit tough to put your faith in."

"I don't trust anyone with a gold front tooth." She crossed the sundeck to inspect the progress of the fire. "Not as bad as it was. It'll probably spare the Old Series

Detectives' Home." When she bent over the railing you could see handprints on the taut seat of her blue slacks.

"You look like a baker's been fondling you, Naomi."

"That's what Huck always says." She rested her palms on her buttocks. "I stand around like this, thinking, while I make bread. Those are my own prints. And usually men who pat behinds go for the more ample ones. Ehrhardt told me that at a cocktail party once."

"He's supposed to be a breast man."

"He'll pat anything, provided it's ample enough."

"Alicia," muttered Levitz.

"On the phone?" Andy started to leave his chair.

"No, no. I was complaining to Cleve about her. You haven't seen the latest issue of *Filmfreak?*"

"She sends me advance copies, but—"

"Anyhow, there's a big spread in there about the cute little beach house Butch Schulz and Tim Argon share down in Malibu."

"So? Everybody knows they're gay."

"Everybody except Cardinal Busino," said Levitz. "Now he's decided Butch isn't right for the part of Pope Pius XII in *Vatican Follies.*"

"I'm sure you can convince the cardinal otherwise." Naomi returned to the kitchen.

"Heck with the cardinal, I've got a call in to Rome." Huck sat. "Wish Butch hadn't posed in the frilly night-gown. That's what set Cardinal Busino off."

"You can't blame Alicia if he—"

"Yeah, I can. I bet you she goaded that simp into those shots."

"About Texas," said Andy. "See in Texas I met . . . well, an absolutely different sort of girl. I don't know . . . what she is, Huck, is honest."

"Honest?"

"You wouldn't think a quality like that could excite you. But she really made an impression on me."

"Is she pretty as well as honest?"

"Oh sure, I don't get interested in anyone who isn't," said Andy. "Frankie is . . . this honesty shines out of her. Boy, it was really very tough lying to her about Jake-2, conning her about Jake Troop's health. I even introduced her to the machine and pretended he was the real Jake." He shook his head. "With Alicia Bramble I don't feel like this, I can plant whatever I have to with her. Frankie, though, is different, and I've been feeling rotten ever since I got home."

"Must be love," said Levitz. "Would this be Frankie Bentin of Four Corners-Mutual Insurance?"

"Right. You know her? She's really special, isn't she?"

Levitz shrugged one shoulder. "That girl will ruin you, Andy."

"What do you mean? What kind of thing is that to tell me?"

"Frankie Bentin happens to be the most honest person I have ever encountered," Levitz told him. "Do you know she's the person, two years back, who got me to admit Wacko Stiltz had a bladder tumor? Yeah, Frankie Bentin of Four Corners-Mutual. We had 6 million lined up to finance *Jack And Jill Went up the Hill* and I go and blurt out that Wacko may only have three months to live."

"Wacko's still alive even today."

"Hindsight," said Levitz. "Stay clean away from that girl. She nearly finished me, Andy. Fortunately I was able to keep Novella from learning I'd been honest with your Frankie. The blame for screwing up the deal fell on the La Brea Medical Center, who Novella came to believe sold Wacko's X rays to FCM Insurance for $12,000."

"Look, I'm in love with Frankie," explained Andy. "That's got to be what it is."

"Nothing wrong with being in love," granted his friend. "I'm only warning you you'll have a hell of a time continuing as a top-notch Stamms-Important agent should you continue entangled with her."

"You admit she's attractive?"

"She's that."

"And she glows with honesty?"

"She does," said Levitz. "Which is the crux of your whole problem."

CHAPTER

FIFTEEN

Honky-tonk piano music was rolling out of the Golden Calf Saloon and into the blazing noonday street. Stepping over cables and wires, dodging wandering propmen and grips, Andy approached the false-front saloon.

Burns Prine, the youthful business manager of Jake Troop, was perching on the hitching rail. He wore sky-blue slacks, a paisley shirt, and an ocher-color neck scarf. Over his head he held a black umbrella. "Huckleburg is still shooting in there," he cautioned Andy.

Leaning against the rail, Andy asked, "How's Jake doing?"

"Brilliantly as usual. The man's one of the great natural actors in the business. We're going to pull down another Oscar for *Saddle Tramp* unless I—"

"I meant his health. We've been on location three days." Andy lifted his wrinkled tennis hat briefly off, wiped at his perspiring forehead with the back of his hand. "And every day Jake looks a bit more slower, more tired."

Prine leaned closer, included Andy in the shade of his umbrella. "Nonsense. You've been spoiled by that android is all. Jake is carrying himself exceptionally well for a man of sixty-one."

"He's sixty-five."

"He's sixty-two. I like to shave a year off, force of habit." He touched Andy's shoulder. "You did, I hear, a marvelous job in Texas. Kept that gadget under control while yet creating enough fights and public disturbances to convince everyone Jake is his old self. Very commendable, and don't think I'm not aware of the sacrifices you made. Being enamored of Alicia Bramble, you naturally must have—"

"We're just friends." Andy pulled away into the glare of the day. "Even if I were goofy over Alicia I wouldn't tell her we pulled off a fraud down there last month."

"I know you're one of the few people at Stamms-Imp with any sort of moral sense. What we did, however, isn't fraud. I checked this out with some very shrewd legal buddies of mine."

"Oh so? 'I've got a Jake Troop robot off passing for him. Is that legal?' Approached them like that?"

Prine smiled. "Credit me with some deftness. I presented a hypothetical case. As yet there simply aren't many laws governing the use of androids and simulacres."

"Conning a bunch of Arab billionaires into thinking Jake's never had a sick day in the past two years, that's still a bunco trick to my way of thinking."

"To your way, yes, but we've already alluded to your exceptional moral sense."

"Vot's der dod-boggled problem?" Oslo Huckleburg shouted inside the saloon.

"Doggone it, Oz," said the real Jake Troop, "will you, for crying out loud, quit interrupting my romantic scenes."

"You ain't no dod-rotted trouble, Chake. But vot's mit you, Skibber?"

"I'm picking up some weird noises on the sound equipment, Mr. Huckleburg."

"Vot kind uff svob-doggled noises, Skibber?"

Skipper replied, "Well, I'm getting a very perceptible whir-whir thunka-thunka razzle-razzle, Mr. Huckleburg."

"Jake's heart," said Andy, starting for the saloon doors.

"Wait now." Prine caught his arm. "We don't want a lot of excitement. I'll handle this, Andy, you wait out here."

He thrust his umbrella into Andy's fingers, went up the plank steps into the Golden Calf.

After a few seconds Andy shut the umbrella, hooked it over the rail, and commenced walking away from the saloon.

A man in a tan jumpsuit, carrying a roulette wheel, nearly collided with him. "Nerfhead," observed the man.

Andy continued on, aimed for the refreshment trailer that was parked on the dry-flat desert beyond the fresh-built Old West street. When he was parallel to the livery stable someone hissed at him.

Novella Stamm was slouched in the driver's seat of a buggy, fanning herself with a copy of *Daily Variety*. She wore a pair of candy-stripe shorts with a matching halter. Perspiration dotted her plump, reddish body. "I heard, unless these old ears deceive me, Oslo's voice raised in complaint. What's wrong?"

Entering the shadowy stable, Andy crossed the crisp, clean straw to climb into the buggy and settle beside his boss. "Jake's heart," he answered.

Novella popped upright, ceased fanning herself. "Another attack?"

"No, probably not. It started making those odd noises again."

"Fully another nineteen days of shooting remain out here. Let us fervently hope Jake lasts that long."

"Last night when I was trying to get to sleep at the motel my heart made a few funny noises I think," he said. "This damn location puts stress on everybody, Novella.

We're going to have to persuade Jake to really take it easy."

"Such will be your task, my lad," said the head of Stamms-Important. "In fact, one is moved to suggest you should be inside the Golden Calf this very moment."

"If we all show too much concern over Jake," said Andy, "it's going to make people suspicious."

Novella resumed fanning herself. "You having curiosity about the progress of the shooting isn't going to arouse anybody."

"Okay, probably not," he said, climbing down out of the buggy. "Another thing, Novella, I saw Jake sneaking out of Tina Verbal's trailer at dawn this morning when I got here."

"Oh everybody sleeps with Tina. It's a tradition."

"Tina Verbal? But she got an Emmy for playing Our Lady of Fatima last season."

"One can win an Emmy and still do what one will with cast and crew."

"Gee, she looks so ethereal."

"Skinny is the more exact word," said Novella. "I would have fancied, cohabiting as you do with the nation's leading movie gossip, that you'd be privy to all the secrets of the trade."

"We're just friends," said Andy, frowning up at his boss from the fresh straw. "Anyway, a lot of that stuff doesn't interest me. I know it should, but . . . do you mean more guys than Jake have . . . been with Tina Verbal?"

"So far it's been Oslo, Flash Fairfield, Milman, and Wishton."

"Wishton? The guy who hands out donuts at the food wagon mornings?"

"That is the very Wishton in question."

"He's only four feet, nine."

Novella shrugged. "Small men are often quite appealing. Years ago, during the filming of *The Teenie Weenies*, I myself . . . You had best go see what's transpiring with dear Jake."

"Tina Verbal . . . she always seemed so distant." Andy went back out into the heat of the day.

———————◆———————

Gumbert was spread out flat on his back on the brown afternoon desert. Arms stretched, ankles crossed, eyes nearly shut. He was twenty-three with crinkly brown hair and a suit of white linen.

"He's into it now," said Snett. He also was twenty-three, with crinkly brown hair and a suit of white linen. He crouched near his partner, a notepad open on one knee.

"Enuff mit der shenanigans," said Huckleburg. "Giff out mit der new scene." He had a polka-dot bandanna tied over his hairless head.

"I see it," moaned the sprawled Gumbert.

"He sees it," Snett said, clapping his hands.

"Doggone if I don't miss old Jim Fargo," said Jake Troop, who was lounging in a canvas chair near his trailer, a striped beach umbrella protecting him from the glare of the declining sun. "He could rewrite a scene faster than greased lightning and still have time for a cordial belt or two."

"I can see it clear." Gumbert's eyes snapped shut.

"Sees it clearly," interpreted his partner.

Andy, drinking a 7-Up from a pseudobottle, was resting with his back against the cowboy star's trailer. He was studying Jake, who was striving to ignore the film's two writers.

"Interior shot," said Gumbert.

"Good, good." Snett scribbled in the book with an electric pencil.

"Saloon," said Gumbert.

"Already ve know it's in der dum-goozled saloon," complained the impatient director.

"You have to let them work this out in their own way," said Burns Prine. "These boys keep winning the awards, Oslo, so they must know what they're doing."

"Monkey-chines," muttered Huckleburg.

"Jake strides over to Tina," said Gumbert.

"Beautiful, beautiful," encouraged his partner.

"Hat-tipping business."

"Tips hat."

"Makes with the grin."

"Grins."

"Not mocking her, but rather conveying compassion and an inner understanding of her plight."

"Perfect."

"Close-up of Tina. We know from her eyes she accepts his honest concern for her."

"Lovely, lovely."

"He speaks. 'What's a nice girl like you doing in a place like this?' "

"Ah," sighed Snett, shutting the notebook, "that's exactly red-letter perfect."

Gumbert sat up, opened his eyes, and smiled with contentment. "This desert country is red-letter perfect for trances. Yow, I could feel the rhythms of the earth loud and clear."

"Sometimes when he goes into a trance in L.A.," explained his partner to the rest of them, "we get too much interference. Once he had one on the Ventura Freeway and all we came up with was trucks shifting gears."

"Made a nice scene for *Little Miss Cheesecake*, though." Gumbert was upright, brushing orange earth from his white suit. " 'Why put a truck scene in the middle of a Sixties Nostalgia number?' some clucks asked. But that scene knocked a lot of smart eastern critics off their towks."

"Is dot der revised scene ve chust heard?" inquired the director.

"I love it." Snett flipped the notebook open. "Want to hear it again?"

Huckleburg shook his head, causing his bandanna to slip sideways. "Chake, vot you tink?"

Jake Troop was absently massaging his chest. "It's

okay, Oz. Done it before, no reason it won't play once more."

"You can't have played a red-letter scene like this before, Jake," said young Gumbert. "Since I only just now created it by tuning my mind to the vibrations of the turning earth and writing down what they revealed."

Jake removed his Stetson, burnished the brim with his elbow. "I don't mind you boys selling me a load of horse manure," he drawled. "But I don't like it when you start shoveling it all over me. Run along now 'fore I forget my vow not to cold-cock anybody this time out."

"No need to get hostile, Jake." Snett shoved the notebook away in an inner pocket of his white suit. He caught his partner's arm, led him off in the direction of their trailer.

"Ve resume shooding in fiveteen dod-gosted minutes." Huckleburg strode away.

Moving next to the cowboy's canvas chair, Andy said, "How're you feeling?"

"How'd you feel if you was paying them two waddies $200,000 for a script?"

"Easy now, Jake," advised Prine. "Gumbert and Snett have a tremendous rep, especially in the Arab world. We'll more than get our investment back from—"

"One of these days I'm going to put Snett in a trance he won't—"

"It's Gumbert who trances," corrected his business manager.

"Maybe I'll cold-cock the pair of them." He gripped the

arms of his chair. "Listen, Burnsy, I want you to fetch James Denver Fargo here to Inferno."

"We don't want to offend Gumbert and Snett. I honestly, Jake, don't think—"

"I'll offend them two twits so good they won't—"

"Relax, Jake. I'll see what I can do."

"Jim Fargo understands how to put together a Jake Troop picture," said the actor. "Take that whole darn business with the greaser this morning. None of that scene of theirs is right."

"Times change."

"Aw horsepucky," said Jake. "Are my fans gonna sit still while I promise a breed to join him in a lettuce boycott? Jake Trooper shoots greasers. And Jim Fargo understands the style I've built up over the—"

"Fargo," put in Andy, "may not be very enthusiastic about coming here."

"Why the heck not, buckaroo?"

"You and he had a misunderstanding down in Drywell."

"We did?" Tongue poking his cheek, Jake nodded his head slowly. "I knew that danged robot was gonna get us all in trouble. How could it impersonate me and at the same time get Jim Fargo riled up? Jim and me go back—"

"Fargo was mad to start with," explained Andy. "He resents not being asked to write *Saddle Tramp* in the first place."

"Well, sir, then he's got to be happy when we ask him to help out now. Send for him, Burnsy."

"Jake, I don't really feel—"

"Get me Jim Fargo or I'll put *you* into a trance, buckaroo."

"Very well, Jake. I'll see what I can work out." Prine shook his head and departed.

"You know what really gives a man heart attacks?" Jake asked Andy. "It's having to work with so many slooping idiots."

CHAPTER
SIXTEEN

Thin yellow light was spreading across the early-morning desert, the distant bluffs and mesas were growing gold around the edges. There was a faintly spicy smell to the air, which fluttered in through the half-open window of Andy's Nezumi sports car. He took a deep breath, yawned.

The dash radio was murmuring. ". . . next all-time

country great hit'll be by Betti Sue Boonfarm. It's that good old classic 'He May Be a Honky-tonk Trucker but . . .'"

"I should have," said Andy to himself, "done something about Frankie Bentin. Called her . . . better yet, gone up to San Francisco to see her."

A large dark bird went flying through the brightening sky. It looked like a vulture.

"Yeah, but if I'd done that, we would have had to talk about Jake Troop. And I really don't—"

Brtzz! Brtzz!

The phone mounted next to his bucket seat had begun to ring. "Yeah?" he said after grabbing up the receiver.

"Do I have it or not?" asked a sultry female voice.

"Have what?"

"You know MCA-Abdullah has been making overtures to me, Andy. It's nice having a cute wiry young agent, but—"

"Nell," he said as he realized which of his clients it was. "Ehrhardt is very interested." Up ahead on the left of the wide flat road loomed the *Saddle Tramp* location camp. "He thinks, and this is a direct quote, you're 'an ideal commando type.'"

"Where's the contract then?"

"I was going to call you today, Nell. You're right at the top of my—"

"We were supposed to have the thing three days ago," said Nell Brinkley.

"Well, Ehrhardt is worried about one thing." Even

though his was the only car on the daybreak road, Andy flicked on his turn indicator. "I'll be talking to him this—"

"One thing? What is it? It can't be my bosom, the way he checked that out."

"Your bosom is fine. Ehrhardt thinks it has just the right blend of appeal and militancy. He's just not completely sold you can put across the leprosy thing. The script calls for a leprous Brazilian commando, remember."

"Andy, you know I spent three frapping months touring leper colonies with the USO. What I don't know about lepers you can stuff in an elephant's heinie."

"That's not quite the right metaphor, Nell. See, an elephant's . . . Oops!" He suddenly saw something strange on the road ahead. "I'll tell Ehrhardt you're very knowledgeable on leprosy, Nell. Get back to you. Bye." He hung up, hit the brakes, and swung his car off the dirt road.

A few seconds ago he'd witnessed Tina Verbal come leaping out of her trailer. She was wearing a man's fringed shirt over nothing else. The flapping shirt had JT branded all over it.

"Tina." He left his car and took off after the running girl.

The slim blonde was heading for the main street of the spurious Western town.

Sprinting, Andy overtook her. "Tina, is something wrong?"

"He's all clammy. He's blue in the face. He's making whir-whir thunka-thunka razzle-razzle noises," the fragile actress explained in gasps.

He got her to stop running. "Jake you mean?"

"I'd advised him a man of his age shouldn't try all those rodeo tricks in bed, but . . . Oh I do think he's dying, Mr. Stoker."

"Okay, get over to Burns Prine's trailer," he instructed the frightened actress. "Tell him you want to see Dr. Faustus and drag—"

"This is hardly the time for literary illusions, Mr. Stoker."

"No, Dr. Faustus is Jake's . . . that is, he's the company doctor. Happens to be sharing a trailer with Burns, who's very demo . . . Get over there, Tina. I'll take a look at Jake." Nudging Tina Verbal onward, he spun and ran back to her trailer.

The noise of Jake's plastic heart was very loud, and it had changed to whir-whir thunka-thunka razzle-razzle sprtz-sprtz. "Doesn't sound good." Andy bounded up into the trailer's bedroom.

The narrow room was dim, smelling of both rose petals and saddle leather. Jake was stretched out on the floor, gnarled hands clutching his middle. He was naked except for boots, spurs, and gunbelt. "Looks like . . . the last roundup . . . buckaroo," he mumbled through pale lips.

"Come on, Jake, you're not going to die in the middle of a picture. That's not like you." Andy yanked a twisted patchwork quilt from the actress's bed, unfurled it, and covered the stricken actor.

"Aw I seen them pearly gates . . . seen 'em clear . . .

shouldn't of tried to diddle her . . . three times in the same . . ."

"Rest, Jake. Dr. Faustus is on his way."

"Plastic ticker . . . dude kind of gadget . . . bury me not on the lone prairie. . . ." His voice faded away.

"Jake?"

The cowboy's imitation heart continued to whir and rattle. The quilt rose and fell over Jake's chest. Andy noticed it was made up of swatches from various pairs of lace panties. He turned away from the unconscious cowboy, waited in the trailer doorway for the approaching doctor.

CHAPTER

SEVENTEEN

"You're not in New Mexico, Mr. Stoker," said the lovely girl with the blue-blond hair.

"Going right back this afternoon, Mona," he told the thirtieth-floor receptionist. "Came back to look out for the interests of my . . ." He noticed a bulky man standing on his head in a corner of the reception room. "Everything is still hanging on that deal, Massacre. Check with me in a week to ten days."

Massacre McMurphy said, "When I get through with my *African Mercenery Diet Book* exercises, Andy, I'm going to bust you in the snoot."

Andy crossed the large snow-white room and squatted beside the upside-down daredevil. "Listen, Massacre, the governor of Colorado loves the idea. There are simply a few little snags which—"

"That's the same as what you handed me last week."

"It's still true."

"The longer we dawdle, the better chance of somebody else doing it. They'll swipe my good idea, the media won't—"

"Who the hell else could have himself shot across the Grand Canyon in a cloud-seeding rocket?"

"And produce rain. That's the clincher," said the headstanding Massacre. "You sure you explained to them the rain part?"

"How did I get ITT's Rainmaking Division interested in sponsoring the special, do you think? Everybody knows about it, Massacre." He straightened up. "Finish your exercises and go home. A week to ten days and we'll be ready to sign papers. Trust me."

"New Mexico must be stimulating," said Mona as he hurried by her boomerang desk. "You look very chipper."

"Yes, I am chipper. That dry desert air is what does it. Your hair looks nice that color."

Mona fluffed it with her fingertips. "You like it better this way than when it was purple?"

"Yeah, it's subtler." He headed down a corridor, concentrating on giving the impression he wasn't going where he was going.

When he passed Gluspan's office the small old agent lowered his *Variety* to call out, "Have you seen the grosses on *I Ate My Grandmother?*"

"Yep, terrific," responded Andy without slowing.

A faint buzzing started in his ears when he neared the office where they had Jake-2 stored. The door hung a good three inches open. Andy ran, pushed into the office. He glanced swiftly around, exclaimed, "Holy nerf!" and shut the door behind him.

There was window glass splashed all over the carpeting, a desk chair lay legs up and, worst of all, the lid of the android's storage case had been ripped off.

Crunching hunks of window underfoot, Andy ran to peer into the crate. It was empty, except for a single silver spur. He picked that up, spun its wheel while studying the damaged room. One of the windows was completely gone, another had an immense zigzag crack across it.

"Is this damn office jinxed? Did that nitwit machine jump, too, just like poor Hoffning?" He went to where the glass had been, stared out and down. Afternoon cars flashed along streets, tiny people hurried. No trace of a fallen robot.

Andy, crunching more glass, uprighted the desk chair

and sat in it. He punched out a three-digit number on the pixphone.

Seconds later the face of Huck Levitz appeared. " . . . no use augmenting them now, Twitchy. Ehrhardt's definitely going to sign Nell Brinkley. . . . Hello."

"Huck," said Andy in a low voice, "could you come in here for a minute?"

"You're not in New Mexico."

"I'm in Hoffning's office."

"Well, I'm sort of tied up with Twitchy Ploog explaining exactly why it's a good thing she didn't get the—"

"Do I have you to thank for my not getting the part, you lopsided gazebo?" Twitchy's lovely gaunt face showed next to Levitz'. "My bosom was good enough for Phelps in *Remembrance of Things Past, Part III*. Isaacson won a special Oscar just for the way he lit it in *Great Gatsby '83*. Now you tell me that cowlike Nell is—"

"Twitchy," cut in Andy, "I've been meaning to tell you something. I was going to pass the news along to Huck but it's much nicer telling you directly. Fossbag would like you for the remake of *Charlie Chan at the Circus*. It's a really splendid part, a bareback rider with a multiple-personality psychosis. You—"

"It doesn't call for enormous breasts?"

"Only average required," replied Andy. "Fossbag told me, 'Acting is what we need for this, my boy, not huge wimpies.' Have Huck set you up to talk to him."

"I'm sorry I referred to you as a lopsided gazebo." Twitchy left the screen.

"Call Fossbag," Andy advised Huck Levitz. "Then it'd be helpful if you could step into this office."

"I'll do it." The screen blanked.

Andy watched the empty phone screen for a half minute before punching out ten numbers.

Lana Woo smiled elatedly when she recognized him. "I was only this moment thinking of you, Andy. This is a gloomy day, exactly perfect for curling up beside—"

"Is the doctor in?"

"No, Andy. Is there something wrong. Your usually cute face seems touched with concern."

"I'd like to talk to Dr. Mackinson. When do you expect him back?"

"No way of telling," answered the exquisite oriental girl. "He's out chasing Leo Gorcey and Ben Franklin, who've run off together. Sometimes he—"

"You people haven't heard from . . . from our cowboy?"

"Why, no. Isn't he with you? I read in the trades location shooting had begun on—"

"That's with the real Jake . . . the real cowboy. Yours we've had in storage. Except now he's . . . no longer in storage."

"There will be times when they get restless," said Lana up in Berkeley. "Take the case of Leo Gorcey and Ben Franklin. An unlikely couple you'd—"

"I'd better start looking for him, Lana. If he does turn up at your place, let me know. Okay?"

"Of course, Andy. I don't suppose you have time to narrate one little ghostly—"

"After I locate him maybe." He hung up, left the chair, and took another peek into the empty crate. When Levitz came into the office he jumped slightly. "You were supposed to be watching—"

"Hey, Fossbag really does want Twitchy. Why didn't you tell me before?"

"Other things on my mind, Huck. Where's Jake-2?"

His friend was staring at the office and the debris. "He's not here."

"So much I figured out on my own. You promised you'd check up on him while I was in Inferno. I came back to get him, find he's jumped out the window right under your nose."

Levitz made a stop gesture with one hand. "Andy, I looked in here when I left Stamms-Important last night. Your android was in his crate, there was no sign of disturbance. I locked the door, departed," he said. "Why do you need the robot?"

"Because Jake Troop's had another heart attack and may not be able to act for a couple weeks. They've got him hidden at a ranch about twenty miles from Inferno," said Andy. "Did you know Tina Verbal was . . . promiscuous?"

"Everybody knows that. Did fooling around with her bring on Jake's latest spell?"

"That and being mad at Gumbert and Snett and insisting on doing most of his own stunts and—"

"Stunts." Levitz poked his shoe toe at the crumbs of broken glass. "Notice how much glass there is in here, and how it's distributed?"

"He broke the window going out."

"Nope, someone broke it coming in. If it was done going out, most of the glass would be way down in the street. This was a stuntman's entrance."

"The Sweetwater Kid," realized Andy. "Is he in town?"

"Yeah, peddling a documentary about Cowboy Heaven."

"Would he steal Jake-2?"

"He didn't have to steal your robot, could be Jake-2 woke up and they decided to go on the town."

"Yeah, like Leo Gorcey and Ben Franklin."

"What?"

"I'll start tracking them," said Andy, moving toward the door. "What time did you check up on him last night?"

"I headed for home about seven. Got tied up with Stooge McAlpin until then. Looks like he's got the part in—"

"Sometime between seven last night and this morning they must have taken off," Andy said. "Obviously if the Sweetwater Kid had come busting in here during working hours today it would have been noticed."

"I've a couple free hours before I have to be at a cocktail party at the *Filmfreak* offices. Want me to help you hunt?"

"I'd appreciate that," said Andy.

CHAPTER

EIGHTEEN

"The wheel of fortune turns in mysterious ways," said Catman, pushing back from the bar and raising his glass to them. "Sure you won't help me celebrate? Even though Stamms-Important didn't lift so much as a little finger to help me, I'm so elated I'm willing to celebrate with anybody."

"No thanks." Andy looked around the large underground room. The decor was intended to suggest a cavern, and all the waiters and bartenders were dressed as trolls. "Have you by any chance see the Sweetwater Kid and . . . Jake Troop?"

"Ask me a more pertinent question," advised Novella Stamms' former butler. "Like what new career triumph I'm in the midst of celebrating."

"Got a new TV part?" inquired Levitz while beckoning to a bartender.

"More than a part, Huck, a series. Can't you guess what from my makeup?"

"The light down here isn't that good." Huck studied Catman's face. "In fact, it makes you seem decidedly yellowish."

Catman chuckled. "I'm supposed to be yellowish," he said. "Also note how I've disguised my eyes to suggest what you call your epicanthic fold. I'm going to be Buddha."

"*The* Buddha?" asked Andy.

"How many are there? I'm going to be the founder of Buddhism in a new thirteen-seg cable series, with options for more. It's an adventure show, with religious overtones. What sold Steinbrunner was my ability with makeup, since Buddha was a master of disguise."

"I never heard that," said Levitz.

"But then you're not exactly a student of Eastern religions," pointed out Catman.

"What'll it be?" A troll bartender was looking across the polished black bar at them.

"We're trying to locate the Sweetwater Kid and a friend of his," Andy told him. "At the Wagon Wheel they suggested the two of them were heading here."

"Those two." Snorting, the troll pointed at the ceiling of the cavern. "Notice that stalagmite up here which—"

"Stalactite," said Andy. "The ones that dangle are known as stalactites."

"You sure?" The bartender frowned. "I've been dressing up in troll garb and coming down here to work for nearly three years and I always thought the stalagmites were the pendulous ones. Son-of-a-gun."

"What about them?" put in Levitz.

"Your buddies shot it down. Yes, Jake Troop and the Sweetwater Kid got to shooting their six-guns at it. Down it came, a goodly chunk of our *ambience*."

"Where'd they go after that?"

"Out of here," said the bartender. "Trolls may be small, but when we all team up we can roust the biggest and the best of them. The gutter is where we heaved those hooligans."

"How long ago?"

"An hour roughly."

"Thanks, we'll see if we can pick up their trail again."

"Had it not been Jake Troop, who I admired in the countless afternoons of my youth, we'd have put the law on them."

"Isn't Jake supposed to be in New Mexico?" asked Catman.

"He had to come back to L.A.," said Andy, "to take care of some personal business. We're all set to go back to Inferno." He assayed a laugh. "You know how Jake is, enjoys his celebrating. Now I have to round him up."

"I enjoy celebrating, too," said Catman. "You don't get tapped to play the Gautama Buddha every day."

"Congratulations," said Levitz, following Andy out of the saloon.

"Do you hear drums?"

"Matter of fact, I do. Is that a good sign?"

Andy slowed, nodding in the direction of the Sunset Strip. "Up that way," he said. "Yeah, I recognize that drumbeat. It's Indians."

They were some 2½ blocks below the Strip, having just inquired after Jake-2 and the Sweetwater Kid at the Sanctified Vegetable Church on Havenhurst. The android and the venerable stuntman had been there a half hour earlier, partaken of the communion of the day, squash today, cried some over their sins, and stumbled out and onward.

Levitz asked, "Rain-dance Indians?"

"Yeah, same as the ones up in Berkeley. Sunshine McBernie must be staging another one of his festivities."

"Well, we didn't catch up with our wandering android at Mechanized Mabel's Brain Massage Parlor or at the

Motel Managers Convention or at the church here," said Levitz. "We may as well check out the rain dance."

"Jake-2 has an affinity for rain dances. He likes to shoot at the Indians."

Blam! Blam!

"Those were shots," said Levitz.

"Yipes, I hope the media isn't around."

"Look." His friend jerked a thumb skyward.

The glowing letters "CBS" were floating through the gathering darkness, flashing from the underside of a television hovercraft.

Andy started to run.

———◆———

" . . . plenty plenty lively here on Hollywood's fabled sleazy sin street the Sunset Strip." A huge man in a spangled jumpsuit was hanging by a rope ladder from an ABC hovercraft. He clutched a mike in his enormous fist. "This is Man Mountain Bushmiller reporting to you live from the scene. Directly below us Sunshine McBernie, looking surprisingly youthful when one considers that his heyday as Little Shoepolish was several decades ago, is leading his band of Indians in a traditional rain dance. The conflict arose when rival rainmakers . . ."

Elbowing through the crowd on the rainbow-lit street, Andy said, "ABC, PBS, NBC, CBS, the Voice of America . . . all here."

"The public never grows tired of riots," said Huck Levitz.

Three hundred assorted people stood watching the activities going on in the middle of the wide street. Fully another hundred, not counting McBernie's Indians, were engaged in battling each other.

". . . midway through McBernie's scheduled rain dance," the dangling Man Mountain Bushmiller was explaining, "dedicated followers of self-styled rainmaker Nosmo Ifkovic arrived on the scene and began trading punches with McBernie's supporters. Carrying an effigy of McBernie and a scale model of one of Ifkovic's cloud rockets, his band of . . ."

"That effigy doesn't look much like McBernie," remarked Andy as a knee in his back thrust him against his friend.

"Effigy is a tough medium to work in," said Levitz. "Besides which, Ifkovic's dedicated followers seem to have ripped the head and right arm off. Hey, there's Jake!"

"Where?"

"Across the street there. See, struggling with the girl who's holding up the tail end of the mock rocket."

"Beating up a girl on national television." Andy used both elbows, fighting to get through the crowd and nearer the conflict.

"Got his six-guns out," said Levitz.

"Then that is what we heard down on—"

Blam! Blam!

"Yep, it was."

Jake-2 had fired two shots up into the night.

Sooty smoke commenced spilling down out of the engine section of the CBS hovercraft.

"Doggone," Jake-2 could be heard to exclaim, "I was aiming at an Injun."

The CBS ship was wobbling, dropping from its hundred-foot altitude to one of less than twenty.

". . . respected colleagues have been sniped by a madman with a gun. With two guns in fact," described Man Mountain Bushmiller. "Wait, ladies and gentlemen, that's no ordinary madman. It is none other than veteran cinema hero Jake Troop. Can he be once again taking an active interest in the politics of the Golden State? Let's see if we can interview the much-loved cowboy actor and find out why he's shooting at . . ."

Kablam! Smash!

The CBS craft slammed into the street.

"He recognized Jake," said Andy, busting clear of the crowd and running a twisting pattern through the dancing Indians. "Why'd that floating bastard have to recognize him?"

"Oof!" Two pro-Ifkovic girls had swung the McBernie effigy and connected with Levitz' stomach. He stumbled to his knees.

Andy kept running. "Hey," he yelled at the android, "quit the damn shooting. *Ars longa, vita brevis!*"

"What an erudite thing to shout at a street fight," observed a scuffling man.

"Jake! Hey!" Andy reached the runaway android caught hold of his arm. "*Ars longa, vita brevis!* You hear?"

The cowboy mechanism shook his head, blinked. "Why, howdy there, buckaroo."

"Your guns. Holster them."

"Sure thing." Jake-2 dropped the two six-shooters into their holsters. "Don't know what got into me. I was snoozing in m'box when all of a sudden there was a horrendous crash and—"

"We're going to get away from here now. Where's the Sweetwater Kid?"

Jake-2 shook his head. "I reckon he's gonna be laid up for a spell."

"You didn't slug that poor old—"

"No, no, pard. We was walking by a glazier's over on Franklin and the Kid got it into his noggin to jump through a window. Well sir, they got like to a hundred great big glass windows lined up inside that there place and by the time the Kid was through No. 6 or 7 he was so woozy he—"

"Okay, okay. We'll forget him," cut in Andy impatiently. "Important thing now is to get you to New Mexico."

"Is my namesake feeling poorly?"

"Yeah, you'll have to replace him. Do you think—"

Boom! Baboom! Rumble!

Thunder sounded, a cool wind came whipping along Sunset. Then it started raining, big fat drops. Falling straight and fast.

"Well sir," said Jake-2 while rain pelted his weathered face, "will you now look at this. This rain-dance stuff really to goodness works. I'm right glad I didn't kill none of them Injuns."

CHAPTER
NINETEEN

"Ah the grandeur of it all, observed Jake-2, filling his mechanical chest with chill dawn air. "Tell you, buckaroo, the good Lord did okay when he made this here part of the world. Take a gander at them distant vistas, the sun peeping over them craggy mesas, the—"

"Silence," said Andy, "is what we need." He'd parked

his Nezumi and was now in the process of leading the exuberant android over to the Jake Troop trailer.

"How can a simple old cowpoke like me keep his dang yap shut when he's confronted with such awesome natural . . . urk!"

"Urk?"

"I stepped in something soft and squishy. It feels like—"

"Morning, Jake."

The mechanical cowboy squinted down, lifted his booted foot off the spread-eagle Gumbert. "Was that you I trod on, Snett? In this thin light I took you for a buffalo turd."

"I'm Gumbert," explained Gumbert as he sat up. "Lucky you didn't injure me seriously, Jake, since I just came up with a revision for the convent scene." He rocked from side to side, got to his feet. "How you feeling?"

"I feel just like a griddleful of sourdough flannelcakes."

"Is that good?" The crinkly-headed writer glanced from Jake-2 to Andy. "Snett's the one who's up on the Western idiom."

"He's in terrific shape," Andy assured him. "After that little bout of indigestion the other evening he—"

"Indigestion? I heard it was a heart seizure. I wish I'd known it was only stomach trouble when I talked to Harlo Glasspants the—"

"You didn't tell Harlo Jake had a heart attack?" Andy caught hold of Gumbert's white lapels.

"A seizure is how I phrased it."

"Is Harlo here?"

"No, he's in L.A. You see, I pix him every other day to tell him what new awards Snett and I have garnered or some whimsical remark I've made or who Snett is nerfing or—"

"Next time you chat, mention it was only indigestion."

"Can you get indigestion from nerfing? I don't do much of it myself, that's Snett's department. Too much slooping detracts, I found, from my trances. Do you want to hear the revise, Jake?"

"Later on, Gummy. Right now I hanker to get me into my trailer and out of these dang boots." He gave the little author a hearty slap on the back, which propelled him into a shaggy joshua tree ten yards away.

While they walked to the trailer Andy said, "I'll have to doublecheck *Hollywood Daily* to make sure Harlo—"

"Aw who's gonna believe that little jasper even if he says I had a seizure? By high noon today ever'body in Hollywood's gonna know Jake Troop was raising heck thereabouts yesterday."

"Maybe," acknowledged Andy, "but once Harlo Glasspants starts to suspect something he's like—"

"The implacable Jouvet of M. Hugo's exemplary tale. Yet I venture to predict we need scarcely—"

"Hey, why are you talking like that?"

Jake-2 blinked, then whacked his temple with the heel of his hand. "Doggone, I keep telling Doc Mackinson he's got to use all new parts or we're gonna have us problems," he said with an authentic Jake Troop grin. "Part of my memory equipment used to be in a George Saintsbury android the doc abandoned. This here Saintsbury feller was one of them English—"

"Never mind. I'll complain to him the next time we talk." He reached up for the door of the cowboy actor's trailer. "Yike!"

The handle turned before he touched it, the door swung outward. "Good morning, Mr. Stoker. Good morning, Jake." Frankie Bentin, the Four Corners-Mutual Insurance Company investigator, stood on the threshold.

"Frankie," said Andy, "it's sure . . . what brings you to Inferno?"

"I was investigating a major fraud case in Albuquerque," replied the red-haired girl. "I decided to swing over here to look in on you people. How are you feeling, Jake?"

The android climbed into the trailer, tossing his sombrero. He kissed the girl on the cheek while patting her left buttock. "Doggone if I don't feel slicker than a spanking new singletree, Miss Frankie. You're looking mighty pretty in that skimpy green dress."

"Thank you. I trust you've been well all these weeks, Mr. Stoker."

"Listen, Frankie, I intended to phone you or probably fly up to San Francisco, but—"

"You wouldn't have found me in. I've been preoccupied with these New Mexican swindlers."

"You must meet a lot of crooked waddies in your line." Jake-2 dropped onto the edge of the bed, began tugging off his boots. "Kind of too bad, a sweet thing like you got to spend so much time looking at the underbelly of society. Dickens, too, knew the lower and lower-middle class of his own day with wonderful accuracy. He could inform this knowledge of his with that indefinable comprehension of man as man that has been so often—"

"Ha ha. Enough kidding around," said Andy with a feigned appreciative chuckle. "Get a little rest, Jake. Oslo's planning to shoot your next scene early this afternoon."

"Might just catch me forty winks at that. Highballing back here from L.A. does make a feller a touch drowsy. Morning to you, Miss Frankie."

Out in the new morning, with the android safely shut inside the trailer, Andy said, "Jake's holding up well on this picture."

"You sound as though you expected otherwise."

"Nope, not me, no. Having been Jake Troop's agent now for several years I know he's a veritable iron man . . . has the constitution of a horse." Andy gestured toward the food trailer. "The chuck wagon should be opening up. Have a cup of soycaf and a sudonut with me?"

"I never eat breakfast."

"Well, let's walk in that direction, anyway."

"I really ought—"

"Frankie, you know what your best quality is? It's your tremendous honesty."

"Most people say it's my eyes."

"Don't spoil it by trying to con me. You must be mad because I never got in touch with you."

"Some, yes."

"I wanted to, but if I had . . . then I would have had to . . . well . . ."

"Had to what?"

"Right at the moment I can't explain it." He put a tentative hand on the girl's bare arm. "I used to be a relatively open—"

"Oh golly!" The back door of the food trailer came popping open. Tina Verbal, wearing nothing save a white waiter's jacket, sailed out.

"There's Tina Verbal," said Andy.

"I noticed," said Frankie.

The fragile actress ran straight to Andy. "Mr. Stoker, I truly suspect I'm a Jonah, a jinx, a—"

"What's wrong, Tina?"

"It's Wishton, he's broken his leg," gasped out Tina. "I cautioned him about attempting to swing from the light fixtures. A trailer is simply too small and cramped for the adequate accomplishment of such things, even for a man of his diminutive stature."

"Better go fetch the doctor, Tina," Andy advised.

"First Jake has a—"

"Touch of indigestion. No need to blame yourself."

"Is that all it was? Indigestion? When I saw him flat out on his bummy with his lips—"

"Indigestion hits different people in different ways. You

run over and ask Dr. Faustus to come take a look at Wishton's ankle."

"Dr. Faustus hasn't been in evidence for the past few days. They brought in a Dr. Anmar from—"

"Oh yeah, that's right. Well, go fetch him."

"I shall." She went barefooting away.

Frankie asked, "Isn't Dr. Faustus Jake Troop's private physician?"

"No," said Andy. "Well, yes. Jake's been sharing him with the cast and crew, showing the kind of big-hearted guy Jake Troop is. Generous and healthy, that's him."

"Why did Jake feel it necessary to bring his personal doctor along at all?"

"Standard procedure, Frankie, you ought to know that." Andy peered into the rear of the food wagon. "How are you getting along in there, Wishton?"

"Groan," replied the caterer.

"Help's on the way," Andy said into the trailer. "Would it be okay if I took a donut?"

CHAPTER
TWENTY

Jake-2 came walking purposefully along the dusty noon-day street.

Fragile Tina Verbal awaited him on the steps of the Golden Calf Saloon. She wore a drab shawl over her gaudy dance-hall girl's costume, had all her worldly belongings done up in a scarlet bandanna, which she clutched to her bosom. "I shan't be exploited and de-meaned any longer, Linn," she said to the broad-shoul-dered cowboy. "And I just know the map my uncle left me will lead us right straight to the Lost Swede Mine."

Jake-2 pushed the brim of his Stetson up an inch with his thumb. "The main points of strictly technical variation in Dumas as compared with Scott are thus the more important use made of dialogue, the greater length—"

"Gut!" cried Huckleburg.

"Saintsbury," muttered Andy.

The director, whose bald head was protected by a ban-danna very much like the one which held all Tina's pos-sessions, stalked around the cameras and equipment. "Ach! Vot's mit you, Chake! You vas acting like a ding-goozled champinzee."

"Right sorry, Oz," apologized the android. "Must of got a bum bottle of ale for breakfast and it's done addled m'brains."

"Dis scene should be a bob-blobbled skinch, Chake! Zo let's giff it—"

"Let me talk to Jake a minute, Oslo." Andy had gone over to stand near the mechanism. "Think I know what the trouble is."

"Hokay. Vot's vun more dod-gasted minute vasted?" He snatched the bandanna from his skull, gave himself several slaps on the head.

Andy tugged Jake-2 down onto the dusty street. "*Ars longa, vita brevis,*" he whispered into one believable ear. "Quit flugging your damn lines."

"Listen, buckaroo, this riles me as much as it does you," confided the android. "I come strolling in all set to spout my lines and instead out come fancy phrases about Shakespeare and the Brand style or the present state of the novel and I feel dumber than—"

"Yeah, but why are you doing it?"

Jake-2 leaned closer. "I hate to say this, buckaroo, but it might be the heat."

"The heat?"

"Doc Mackinson is, we all got to agree, a man of genius. Howsoever, he ain't worked out every single kink in this simulacre dodge."

"You mean when the day is exceptionally hot your memory mechanism—"

"Makes me talk a little loco."

"Can Mackinson tell me how to fix it?"

"Ain't nothing to fix. What we probably ought to do, buckaroo, is wait till it cools off."

Andy, glancing over his shoulder at the angry director, said, "I doubt he's going to want to hold up shooting till late this afternoon."

"Well sir, then we got to just keep muddling through."

"Dot's no dod-boggled minute," shouted Huckleburg while rearranging his bandanna, "dot's a ding-foozled gonverence!"

"Back me up on whatever I tell him," Andy instructed the mechanical man.

When he walked by Tina, the fragile actress said, very

quietly, "I hope his poor old brains aren't addled because of last night."

"Last night?"

"I really hadn't intended to have any further inter-course with Jake after the way he turned blue and had in-digestion the last time," said Tina. "But last night, with the full desert moon shining bright on cactus and forlorn joshua tree I—"

"You shouldn't be sleeping with that . . . never mind. Don't feel guilty about it, Tina."

"Now it giffs a dum-baggled gonverence mit der pean-bole hactress!"

Andy, swallowing once, went down the saloon steps to face the director. "Sunstroke," he said.

"Vot?"

"Nothing serious, a very mild case of sunstroke is what Jake has. Happens now and then, not often since Jake is in such terrific shape, but it does happen. I recall once when he was in Ariz—"

"Zunztroke? Is dot vhy dis dummox can't giff vun dum-gozzled line straid?"

"He'll be in tip-top shape in a couple hours, Oslo," Andy assured the director. "Maybe you can shoot around him or—"

"Shood around him? Und who stants on der dod-rotted steps mit Tina, his ding-rusted horse? Already it giffs grazy Arabs gumplaining ve iss goink offer der pudget unt now you—"

"Oz, old buck," put in Jake-2, "this ain't the first movie

picture we made together by a long shot. You know dang well the Trooper never let nobody down for long. Call it quits now and I'll be back in the saddle by four this afternoon."

"Tree."

"Okay, three." Jake-2 tipped his hat to Tina and sauntered out of the scene.

"Find him," urged Andy.

"I don't have to locate him, Andy, I know where he is," said Lana Woo from the pixphone screen. "He's down in the well with Huntz Hall."

"Haul him out then. Why's he in a well?"

"The Dead End Kids—did I tell you our Mafia client canceled his order for them and wants the Little Rascals instead, so we have a nice set of near-perfect Dead End—"

"Never mind, I don't want to know why Dr. Mackinson and Huntz Hall are at the bottom of a well. . . . Listen, Lana, Jake-2 . . . our mutual cowboy friend claims the sun makes him a little goofy. Is that possible?"

"Oh." Lana's lips parted slightly, she rubbed her fingertips over her lovely chin. "How hot is it exactly where you are?"

"A hundred and four degrees."

"Oh."

Andy waited out a few seconds of silence. "So?"

"We did have some trouble once with a Brazilian dictator simulacre we made. On very hot days in Rio he started reciting the wisdom of Thomas Paine. Fortunately he recited in English, so his image as a ruthless dictator wasn't spoiled. I know Dr. Mackinson tried to compensate for the heat factor, since Jake Troop acts in so many hot outdoor—"

"I won't even go into the morality of allowing a machine to rule a country, even a shabby country like Brazil," said Andy. "No, what I want to get down to, Lana, is how can we keep this from happening any further with Jake-2? *Saddle Tramp* is already four days behind schedule."

"Do you have him handy?"

"Yeah, I brought him here to my cabin at the Cisco Kid Motor Inn."

"What is the status of your real cowboy? Could he possibly fill in for a day while I fly out to you to see—"

"Won't work, Lana. They haven't let me see Jake since I got back from L.A., but I'm fairly certain he's . . . well, not in any shape to act."

Lana bit her lower lip, thoughtful. "Okay, let me talk to him," she said finally. "I may be able to do something with one of the doctor's remote hypnocontrol gadgets. If I can find it."

"What do you mean, 'If I can find it'?"

"Things are a bit bohemian here, Andy, which surely you remember," answered Lana. "There's a certain amount of eclectic clutter, but—"

"How big is the gadget you have to find?"

"It's about the size of a bread box with knobs and lights all along the—"

"Go hunt, we'll wait."

"I spied a young cowboy all wrapped in white linen," sang Jake-2 from the rough-hewn wooden chair facing the blank television set. "All wrapped in white linen and cold as the—"

"No singing."

"Ain't that better than literary criticism?"

"This is a very sedate motel. I don't want us getting tossed out before Lana can—"

"Haw haw," laughed Jake-2. "Whiles you was parking that dinky Nip car of yours the manager offered to sell me the favors of his thirteen-year-old daughter."

"Well, he's a little starstruck. People do strange things when they meet movie stars," said Andy. He sat staring anxiously at the pixphone screen.

"I wonder if I might ask you a few questions about American foreign policy?" Secretary of State Fassbarker was on the phone screen. "We want all Americans to participate in our government, to feel they are involved in every decision be it—"

"Get back in your crate," suggested Andy. "Geeze, why do they let so many of you gadgets run around loose? It's—"

"I beg your pardon, young man." Fassbarker was scowling. "What gave you the notion I was—"

"I found it, Andy." Lana gently pushed the Secretary of State out of the field of vision. "You can wait down in the parlor, Mr. Secretary."

"Was that really Fassbarker? I thought it was the android Dr. Mackinson showed me when—"

"You're not supposed to know about it. Best not say any more or you'll have the National Security Office or the Federal Police or—"

"Talk to Jake-2," Andy said. "If he keeps acting bizarre they're going to conclude he's goofy, which is just as bad as being physically ill."

"Ask him to come close to the phone screen." Lana held a light-encrusted box in front of her.

"Talk to Lana," Andy told the android.

Jake-2 ambled over to oblige. Settling in the chair in front of the pixphone table, he tipped his sombrero. "Howdy, Miss Lana. You're looking pretty as the tail feathers of a mourning dove."

"Watch the top row of lights," instructed the girl. "Watch very closely. As you watch, repeat these words: 'I am not a British literary critic, I am cowboy. I am not a . . .'"

CHAPTER
TWENTY-ONE

"That's not Jake Troop!"

Andy spun around, spotted the thin old man standing at the edge of the crew on the late-afternoon street. Apparently no one else had caught the muttered charge. Hurrying to him, Andy very quietly said, "Welcome to New Mexico, Mr. Fargo."

On the steps of the saloon Jake-2 was going through the scene with Tina Verbal which he'd fluffed this morning. He was sticking to the script.

"What the hell's going on?" said James Denver Fargo. "That galoot's no more Jake Troop than I am."

Andy eased the old screenwriter farther from the filming. "Drive out here in an open car, Mr. Fargo? Probably got a touch of sunstroke. Lot of it going around. Matter of fact—"

"You're the punk who was with him in Drywell. Get your mitts off me."

"Jake's going to be very pleased having you here," said Andy, moving Fargo even farther along the street. "Don't upset him by—"

"Sensed something fishy down in Texas." Fargo rubbed at his bloodshot eyes. "That wasn't Jake either. Jake Troop wouldn't have high-hatted me."

"The motion-picture industry is always in flux. Sometimes Jake may strike you—"

"Quit bulling me, punk. That man isn't Jake Troop," Fargo said. "He don't move like Jake, he don't even talk like him. I've been a close friend of Jake's for more than forty years and I know he—"

"Of course it's Jake Troop," insisted Andy. "I mean, here we are in the middle of filming a Jake Troop picture. Obviously you can't make a Jake Troop picture without Jake Troop; ergo—"

"You can't bull me with punk logic," said Fargo. "What I want to know is why that ringer is—"

"What seems to be the trouble, Jim?" Burns Prine joined them, lowering his black umbrella and shutting it.

"No wonder you punks didn't want me on the film. You're pulling some kind of fast shuffle here and—"

"Jim, you're a very perceptive fellow," said Prine, smiling. "If you'll take a little ride with me I believe I can explain everything to your satisfaction."

"That doesn't seem likely, punk."

"Give us a chance to put your mind at ease. I know that's what Jake wants," Prine went on. "We're counting on you to turn this picture into another Jake Troop box-office smash. I'd like you to come along, too, Andy."

"What good's taking a ride going to do?" Fargo wanted to know. "You're trying to hoodwink me into—"

"You come along, Jim," promised Prine, "and I'll let you talk to the real Jake Troop."

"Why have you been crying?"

"It's an allergic reaction. I'm allergic to cactus."

"Nobody's allergic to cactus," said Andy.

"When one takes it in the form of tequila a wide range of reactions are possible, my lad," said Novella Stamms.

Andy and his chunky boss were sitting on the wide front porch of the ranch house Jake Troop was recuperating in. Dusk was spreading across the flat desert country, a windmill at the property edge was creaking as it slowly spun in the warm night wind.

"Something's wrong," persisted Andy.

"Jake is ill, nothing more."

"You don't cry very often, Novella. The last time I saw you cry was when Bilbo & Chuck crashed in the Azore Islands."

"I sobbed a little, there were no tears. Losing a second-rate ventriloquist client and his moderately repulsive dummy don't make one—"

"Another thing, Novella. Why did Burns Prine drag that old hack Fargo out here?"

"Fargo is far from being a hack. There are scenes in *Last Stage to Paso Robles* that are touching as well as—"

"Jake's worse. Is that it? We're going to have to use Jake-2 longer than anticipated and you want to persuade Fargo to—"

"Jake is fine. I'd venture to predict we won't be needing the android much beyond the end of this week."

Andy pointed at the closed front door of the ranch house. "One more odd item. All the Tumbleweed Boys are very quiet tonight. Even old Crabby is subdued. You can hardly hear—"

"Punks! What kind of phonies are—"

Crash! Wham!

Andy jumped to his feet. "That was Fargo."

"Sit," advised his boss.

"Those Tumbleweed Boys are pretty tough, for a retired Western singing group. They shouldn't be picking on that old guy if that's what—"

"Sit."

Andy sat. "You already know what's going on in there, don't you? Burns told you before he took—"

"Jim Fargo will simply become a guest here."

"Against his will?"

"Judging from the sounds issuing from within, Andy, that seems a fair surmise."

"He realized Jake-2 is a fake. So you're going to keep him out of the way until *Saddle Tramp* is finished."

"Exactly."

"Novella, it's one thing to bring in a robot ringer. When you start locking up veteran screenwriters, though, that's kidnaping."

"One assumes Fargo will come around in time. Until he does, we'll store him in the cellar. There's quite a substantial cellar below this establishment."

"Yeah, but you lured Fargo out here to talk to the real Jake," said Andy. "You ought to let Jake talk the old guy into keeping quiet."

"That is no longer a valid possibility."

"Why?"

"Jake Troop died five hours ago."

CHAPTER
TWENTY-TWO

A neon cowboy and his mount were bouncing endlessly in the night sky. Below the team floated the words "The Last Roundup Motor Lodge."

Andy swung his sports car off the road, drove beneath the illuminated adobe arches of the motel. He parked in the visitor lot and stayed sitting in the car for several minutes. When he climbed out the night wind worried at him, making his jacket billow and flap.

He stood on the cement-door step of Cabin 6 almost a full minute before knocking.

Light glowed at all the shaded windows of the adobe cottage but no one came to the door.

Andy knocked again, louder.

This time the door was opened. Frankie Bentin smiled out at him. "I was thinking about you," she said, "wondering if you'd ever get around to dropping by for a visit." The girl had her hair wrapped in a sea-green towel, was wearing a short terry robe.

"Want to talk," he said, still on her threshold.

"Come on in," she invited. "If you'll sit for a few minutes I'll get some clothes—"

"This is somewhat urgent." The night wind blew the cottage door shut an instant after he'd entered her living room.

"Okay, we'll talk right now." She nodded at a sunburst sofa as she seated herself, bare legs tucked under, in a wood and neoleather chair. "You look upset."

"I haven't been," said Andy, forgetting to sit down, "completely honest with you. Tonight Burns Prine and Novella Stamms made me an offer. An impressive piece of money."

"That didn't cheer you up?"

"It's what I have to do for the money. Did you ever read any books by John P. Marquand? Don't suppose you have, nobody does anymore. My father had some of them stored in our basement and . . . well, the point is they offered me a percentage of *Saddle Tramp* and all subsequent Jake Troop pictures. What I have to do, all I have to do, is keep quiet."

Frankie slowly unwound the towel from around her head, very gently began to rub her damp red hair. "Keep quiet about what, Andy?"

"Several things." He sat down finally, put his hands on his knees, moved them, returned them to his knees. "What do you know about robotics?"

"I guess people in robotics make robots."

"Up in Berkeley is a guy named Dr. Jack Mackinson." Andy looked everywhere but at the red-headed girl. "A few months ago he constructed an android which was an exact replica of Jake Troop. That android, Jake-2 we call him, is who went to the opening of Cowboy Heaven. The Jake you met was a mechanical man."

"I met Jake Troop. I can't believe—"

"Nevertheless, Frankie, that was an android, a very convincing one. Most of the time, when he isn't leaking oil or quoting Saintsbury," said Andy. "The reason we used him is because Jake Troop, the real Jake, has been ill for weeks. All the rumors about heart attacks are absolutely true."

"And who's here in Inferno starring in *Saddle Tramp?*"

"Initially it was the actual Jake, but then he had another attack and I had to bring Jake-2 back. We had the machine stored in the Stamms-Imp offices. All the stuff in the media about Jake Troop shooting down network cameras and participating in rain dances . . . well, they're talking about Jake-2."

"A fraud," said the insurance investigator.

Nodding, Andy continued, "The reason they made me the offer tonight . . . Jake Troop is dead."

Frankie pressed her hand to her breast. "Then it's all over, isn't it?"

"No, it's not," he replied. "I figured it would have to be, too. Then Novella and Burns pointed out that everybody will lose a good deal of money if *Saddle Tramp* isn't completed. Okay, so we have a perfectly believable android here who can finish the film without anyone, except old James Denver Fargo, being any the wiser. Fargo's the old screenwriter they've got locked in the cellar out at—"

"Locked in the cellar?"

"That's another thing that bothers me, Frankie. I mean, I can go along with a fraud I suppose, to a certain point. But when you start locking old men in cellars and putting dead men on ice—"

"Is that what they're going to do with Jake Troop's body?"

"Dr. Faustus has a way to freeze it. When they finally decide to let Jake Troop officially die they'll thaw him out. Dr. Faustus is getting a percentage of the *Saddle Tramp* gross."

"After *Saddle Tramp* is in the can, will they let Jake die?"

"That was probably the original plan, but then Novella and Burns got to thinking," said Andy. "Why stop with this picture? Jake Troop's probably good for a picture a year for the next five or six years. That's a lot of money, especially if they have Jake's salary to split among themselves. The android, you know, works for nothing." He stood up, sat down, stood up. "I shouldn't have gone along with all this even as far as I did. Now, though, I just have to quit. What they plan to do, it's simply not right."

"No, it isn't."

"I came to you, since you're about the only really honest person I know. You've got the facts now, so you can get in touch with your company and whatever legal authorities have to be brought in."

"You came to me first with this?"

"Of course, Frankie. Who else could I confide in?"

She left the chair, retied the belt of her robe. "They're shooting some night stuff for *Saddle Tramp* tonight, aren't they?"

"The brawl scene, yeah."

"Okay, Andy, let me make a call to San Francisco," she said, "and then drive back to the location."

"Back there?"

"You don't want any of them to get suspicious. By tomorrow morning everything will be out in the open and you can pack up and depart."

"Then start hunting for a new job."

"Someone with your integrity won't have much trouble," she assured him. "In fact, I can probably do something for you." She came close to him, kissed him once on the cheek. "Wait here until I make my call." The red-haired girl went into the kitchen, closing the door after her.

But a faint gust of wind came drifting through the cottage at that moment and kept the door from shutting completely. It stayed about four inches open.

Which is why Andy was able to hear what Frankie was saying on the pixphone.

" . . . to me first. No, he's not going to keep quiet. . . ."

Feeling all at once very cold, Andy got up and moved closer to the opening.

" . . . and how come, Burns, this Faustus gets a percentage of the gross and I only get a percentage of the *net*? I was on to you as far back as Drywell, and I could have spoiled your hoax anytime since then. I still can unless—"

"We can negotiate that, Frankie," came the voice of Jake Troop's business manager. "Right now we have to keep Andy from screwing us up. We'll have to grab him, toss him in with Fargo."

"I'm sending him back to the location camp. You can . . ."

It's possible to run silently. If you concentrate, you can do it.

Andy was out of the cottage, back in his car in less than a minute. He turned on the engine, backed out of the lot, and went roaring off. Not toward the *Saddle Tramp* location, but toward his own motel.

CHAPTER
TWENTY-THREE

He saw the gun first, a .38 pistol. Saw it before he noticed Burns Prine's smiling face. "We better have a chat, Andy," said the affable young man, extending the pistol across the threshold and into Andy's motel cabin. "A friendly talk, nothing more. I really believe you're nowhere near as stupid as old Fargo. We can work out a better percentage for you, a larger—"

Wham! Whap!

Andy had slammed the door on Prine's wrist.

"Yow!" Prine's fingers starred out and the gun dropped.

Catching it, Andy spun and dashed across the room. He ignored the suitcase he'd been packing and shouldered out the rear door of the place.

Some sort of prickly bushes tripped him. He went sliding on his knees across the gray ground. Getting himself upright, he ran around the cabin to the place where his Nezumi sports car was parked.

Two burly men were standing, backs to him, a few yards in front of the car. Tumbleweed Boys, judging by their size.

He snuck into the driver's seat, shut the door with no sound. When he started the motor the Tumbleweed Boys stiffened, turned, and came charging at the front of the auto.

Andy tromped on the gas pedal and went bowling ahead, scattering Tumbleweed Boys as he did. He was already on the highway before the two cars they'd come in shot out of the motel grounds in pursuit.

"Frankie," he said to himself, "the only honest-looking girl I ever met. The only girl who ever inspired me to admit I'd been conning people. Nerf."

A side road appeared on his right. He spun off onto it, his car rocking and squeaking just like a cop series car.

A narrow, bumpy road. He had no idea where it led.

He was determined to outrun them. His foot pushed down harder on the gas pedal.

In the rear-view mirror he could see two pairs of bobbing headlights. They were on the side road, about a quarter mile behind him.

The distance separating him from Burns Prine, the Tumbleweed Boys, and whoever else remained the same for the next bumpy several miles.

Then his Nezumi commenced making noises. "Whir-whir thunka-thunka," it said. "Razzle-razzle."

"A heart attack. My car's having a heart attack."

"Whir-whir thunka-thunka razzle-razzle sprtz-sprtz."

The pursuing car lights grew larger and larger.

His car had stopped dead.

After two futile tries at getting it to start, Andy left the car. He'd covered twenty feet when he remembered the pistol. He snatched it off the passenger seat, went running off the road and into the night desert.

The cactus plants were man-high and rising all around him, prickly black shapes in the clear windy night.

"Buildings," he said.

A half mile ahead of him was a clump of dark buildings. Some little town that didn't exist anymore, a ghost town.

Andy discovered he was running along an old dirt road that must lead straight into the abandoned town. There was a good deal of dust rising, and the wind was forcing it into his mouth, his throat, his lungs.

"Not used to running. Ought to start a sensible exercise program when I get home. If I get home."

No, they wouldn't kill him. Nothing like that. Only proposition him.

He was in the middle of the one-street town now. He halted, sucking in air through his mouth.

One of the old structures seems more substantial than the others. Built of adobe brick, with a sturdy wooden door still in place. It had been a feed store once; there were still splotches of Purina checkerboards gracing its front.

Andy stumbled inside, shut the door.

A snake went slithering across the dirty plank floor, up and out the glassless front window.

"Andy," called Burns Prine, "there's no need for all this exertion."

"Quit babying the guy," said one of the Tumbleweed Boys. "Let's beat the pucky out of him!"

Andy studied the pistol, fiddled with it until he decided it was ready to fire. He stuck it out the window, aimed high, and squeezed the trigger.

Blam!

"Hey, he's got a gun!"

"Of course he does. He managed to wrestle mine away from me."

"May one offer a sensible suggestion, Andy?"

"Novella!" So she was out there, too.

"We all know what a shame it would be for you to languish in a cellar for weeks and weeks," called his boss through cupped hands. "None but that old schmuck for companionship. Therefore, consider a new offer. I will remove Jake Troop from your client list at once, provide you with—"

"Remove him? Fate's done that."

"He's waxing philosophical," complained another of the burly Tumbleweed Boys.

"I'll give you our most successful and even-tempered clients to manage."

"And I," shouted Burns Prine, "will make you a full vice president in Trooper Productions."

"I'll," offered Novella, "move you into Hoffning's office, where there's eight square feet more floor space than your present office provides."

Blam!

"Not interested," Andy told them after the sound of his second shot had faded. "Only interested in spreading the truth."

"Twenty-five per cent of all European leasing money on *Saddle Tramp*," called Prine.

"Your own soycaf machine in your office," shouted Novella.

"Go away. I'll start aiming lower if everybody doesn't depart."

"No you ain't, little pal."

Andy hadn't been aware of the back door until the largest of the Tumbleweed Boys came through it carrying a sawed-off shotgun.

"It's a standoff," said Andy. "You shoot me, I shoot you."

The big man with the shotgun chuckled. "One slug fired by a dude like you ain't going to do as much to me as a couple barrelsful of pellets'll—"

"Well, possibly you've got a . . ." Andy didn't finish the sentence. He heard something out there in the night.

Hoofbeats of an approaching horse.

CHAPTER
TWENTY-FOUR

Blam! Blam!

"I hardly ever miss, buckaroo." Jake-2 stood in the rear doorway, twin six-guns smoking in his hands.

"Ow! Yowie!" The Tumbleweed Boy, his shotgun blasted from his grip, was hopping around waving his wounded hands in the air.

"No time for palaver, Andy. We got to hightail out of here." He went back out into the night.

Andy followed.

Jake-2 was already in the saddle of his black stallion when Andy emerged from the old feed store. "Hop on behind me, pard."

"Never done much riding, and I'm—"

"Get on up afore the rest of them waddies realizes what's transpired and come hotfooting 'round back here." The android leaned, aided Andy into the saddle. "Giddyap, buckaroo."

The powerful horse started galloping across the night desert, away from the ghost town and from Burns, Novella, and the others.

"How'd you know I was there?" asked Andy.

"Odd things been going on tonight. All them galoots stopping by the location camp to gather up real shotguns and all. I got it in my mind to see what was in the wind," said Jake-2. "Didn't make Oz too cordial when I vamoosed in midbrawl. I figure, though, that's what pards are for."

"You sensed I was in trouble?"

"Knew somebody must be, guessed you was the most likely candidate."

"You shouldn't rescue me, actually," said Andy as they galloped along sharing the saddle. "We're not on the same side anymore."

"Aw, I know what Novella and Burnsy got in mind for me. But I also know you been developing a late-blooming sense of honesty. Which is what's been getting you in trouble."

"Yep, it has."

"Way I see it, I wouldn't be much of a Western hero if I was on the side of Mammon all the time," said Jake-2.

"Well, I appreciate your help."

They had reached another roadway and up ahead was a small gas station with its lights still on. A pixphone booth glowed pale yellow at the edge of the station grounds.

"Next question we got to answer, buckaroo, is what are—"

"Stop at this station, Jake. Near the phone."

"Sure thing, pard. Whoa there, whoa, big feller."

The station attendant, a frail young man, stayed inside his office. "We don't do horses. Mostly cars is—"

"Want to use the phone." Andy scrambled down off the stallion.

Inside the booth he tucked the pistol into the waistband of his trousers, then shoved a charge card into the slot of the pixphone.

"Proceed," invited the voice of the phone.

Andy punched out a Los Angeles number.

"Well, what a nerfing surprise." Alicia Bramble, unclad and hunkered in her enormous pink bed, frowned at him. "I didn't think you even knew my number any—"

"Be silent for a moment, Alicia," he said. "I have an item for you."